
"Why didn't you do something?"

Amy whirled around to face a dark-haired boy about her own age dressed in work-stained jeans. "Me?" she stammered in confusion.

"I don't see anyone else around here, do you?" His blue eyes blazed in indignation.

"But I don't know anything about horses!"

"It doesn't take much knowledge to flap your arms and turn the animal back! Now I'll probably have to chase her heaven-knows-where!" He glared at Amy, a frown creasing his brow. "What are you doing here anyway? Who are you?"

Amy drew herself up proudly. "I'm Amy Longeway, Mr. Thompkin's stepdaughter. . . ."

Dear Readers:

Thank you for your many enthusiastic and helpful letters. In the months ahead we will be responding to your suggestions. Just as you have requested, we will be giving you more First Loves from the boy's point of view; and for you younger teens, younger characters. We will be featuring more contemporary, stronger heroines, and will be publishing, again in response to your wishes, more stories with bittersweet endings. Since most of you wanted to know more about our authors, from now on we will be including a short author's biography in the front of every First Love.

For our Book Club members we are publishing a monthly newsletter to keep you abreast of First Love plans and to share inside information about our authors and titles. These are just a few of the exciting ideas that First Love from Silhouette has in store for you.

Nancy Jackson
Senior Editor
Silhouette Books

DON'T FENCE ME IN
Brenda Cole

First Love from Silhouette
Published by Silhouette Books New York
America's Publisher of Contemporary Romance

First Love from Silhouette by Brenda Cole

Alabama Moon #60
Larger Than Life #79
Don't Fence Me In #119

SILHOUETTE BOOKS, a Division of Simon & Schuster, Inc.
1230 Avenue of the Americas, New York, N.Y. 10020

Distributed by Pocket Books

ISBN: 0-671-53419-X

First Silhouette Books printing November, 1984

10 9 8 7 6 5 4 3 2 1

America's Publisher of Contemporary Romance

Printed in the U.S.A.

RL 5.6, IL age 11 and up

DON'T
FENCE ME IN

1

Amy wandered aimlessly around her empty room. She paused to glance out of the window, where the sun was still shining brightly on the subdued pastel colors of San Francisco. Out there, everything looked normal; only when she let her gaze drift back inside was she reminded that her world had been turned upside down.

She swallowed past the lump in her throat. There had been so many changes in the last few years. First there was the death of her father, and then the difficult move from their home in the suburbs of Palo Alto to an apartment in the city so they would be closer to her mother's new job and Amy's grandmother.

But eventually she had adjusted. In fact, she had come to love the sights and sounds of this unique city, with its hills, cable cars, and varied mixture of people. After the first year of feeling like an outsider, she had finally settled in at school and had her own network of friends, a curious combination of the sophisticated country club set from her own neighborhood and the street-smart crowd of the inner city.

What had finally clinched her place in the crowd had been the fact that she, Amy Longeway, had managed to attract the attention of the most sought-after boy in school, Stephen Kemp. It hadn't been easy, either. She had practiced being elusive and mysterious. She had changed her looks and behavior every week. She pretended to be busy when he finally called her for a date. She managed to appear at every party, movie or sports event that he attended.

But none of that mattered now, for she would have to begin all over again in a new town, a new school, and with a whole new set of problems. A hot tear escaped her eyelid and trailed down her cheek. It just wasn't fair!

Her mutinous thoughts were interrupted by a soft knock at the door. Her mother, looking excited and happy, poked her head into the room. "Are you ready?"

Quickly, Amy wiped the tear away. "I suppose so. With everything already packed and loaded on the moving truck, there's not exactly a lot left to do," she said without attempting to hold back any of the bitterness she felt.

A look of concern clouded her mother's eyes, and at the moment Amy didn't care that she had caused it. "We'll wait for you downstairs," her mother said softly.

By "we," Amy knew her mother meant her and Dick Thompkins, her new husband. Personally, Amy had nothing against Mr. Thompkins. In fact, until she learned that her mother's marriage to him would mean moving away from San Francisco to his ranch some three hundred miles away, Amy had highly approved of him. But now . . . She sighed heavily and, with a feeling of despair, looked around the room to say a final good-bye before closing the door.

She found her mother and Mr. Thompkins in the living room. They were standing close together, their heads barely inches apart, his arm around her mother's waist. They looked perfect together, and she envied them their happiness.

Amy stood watching them from the hallway until Dick noticed her. "I have an idea," he said with a smile that was meant to include her. "Why don't I take you two out to a fancy restaurant before we leave the city? Any place you want to go."

"I'm not hungry." Amy said shortly.

"But you have to eat, and I think we should make a celebration out of it," her mother said placatingly.

"Since we have to go, I'd rather just get it over with. I don't see any reason to celebrate," Amy said. She was tired of them treating this move as though it were an exciting adventure for everyone.

Dick cleared his throat. "Maggie," he said. "Would you mind if I talked to Amy alone?"

"She's just upset, Dick," Maggie said hesitantly, looking from her husband to her daughter. "She'll be all right. You'll see."

"I always am, aren't I?" Amy added sarcastically.

Maggie bit her lip and looked helplessly at Dick.

Amy felt a stab of remorse and had to steel herself to keep from apologizing. In the difficult times after her father's death, she had become very protective of her mother and she didn't really want to hurt her now, but she had to make them see what they were doing to her.

Dick squeezed Maggie's shoulder. "You go wait in the car. It'll be all right. I promise."

With a last pleading look at Amy, her mother left the room, tears glistening in her eyes.

Now that she was alone with Dick, Amy stared at him defiantly. She knew her behavior had been insolent, but silently she dared him to reprimand her. After all, she did have a right to her own feelings.

But Dick took his time before saying anything. He looked

at Amy curiously; not agitated as her mother had been nor angry as she had expected, just interested. "Amy," he finally asked, "what exactly is bothering you? Our marriage? Me? The fact that your mother and I eloped without telling anyone?"

In spite of her resentment, Amy tried to be honest. "No. I'm glad Mama's happy again and I don't have anything against you. But why doesn't anyone consider what I want?"

"You don't want to move?"

"Do you blame me? I'll have to leave all my friends, and grown-ups just don't understand how hard it is to make new friends and fit in with another crowd."

"You know I have a daughter too. She'll help you."

His reminder didn't reassure Amy at all. It just brought up another fear. "And what if we don't like each other? After all, I'll be moving into her house, her school, and her crowd."

Dick seemed to consider this. At least he didn't imply that simply because she and his daughter Lisa were the same age, they would automatically like each other, and he didn't tell her, as her mother had done, that if she had a positive attitude, everything would work out.

"What do you want us to do?" he asked patiently. "I can't change the fact that my ranch is near Truckee or that I have a sixteen-year-old daughter."

"I could stay in San Francisco and live with Grandmother," Amy made the suggestion in desperation.

"Do you think your mother would be happy moving away without you? Could you be happy without her?"

"I don't know," Amy cried, "I just know that I don't want to move again."

"What about this? What if you come with us now, give the ranch and Lisa a chance, and if you are still unhappy there when summer's over, if you *really* don't like it, I'll see what I can do to get Maggie to let you stay with your grandmother during the school year."

It was the first hope she had allowed herself. "Really? You'd let me come back here to go to school?"

"If you agree to give the ranch a fair chance and try to make things easier for your mother," Dick said. "But if you continue behaving like a spoiled child, I'll have to concede that you aren't mature enough to decide where you should live."

Amy blushed hotly. She knew she hadn't been very far from throwing herself on the floor, kicking her feet, and refusing to move. But all she had wanted was for them to take her problems seriously. "I promise I'll try, and thanks for understanding."

Dick grinned. "Well, I do have a teenager too."

Amy returned his smile shyly. He really was a nice person. She wouldn't mind living with him if he lived in San Francisco. Of course, he couldn't take the place of her real father, but he was an acceptable substitute, and it would be nice to have someone to share the responsibility of keeping her mother happy. "By the way," she asked, "what am I supposed to call you?"

"I usually answer to Dick," he said to her relief.

As they loaded their suitcases and drove away from the city, Amy tried to keep up her spirits by reminding herself that this move wasn't permanent—at least not for her. By September, she would be back at Bay View High School having pajama parties with her friends after the ball games, trying out for the tennis team and, with a little luck and some hard work, going to the junior prom with Stephen Kemp.

But as the hours crawled by and the car began the laborious climb up into the Sierra Nevadas, the mountain range that lined the inside border of California and separated it from Nevada, she found it harder and harder to concentrate on September when she still had the whole summer to get through. Her mother tried to help pass the time by asking Dick to tell them about the ranch.

Since Maggie had visited the ranch with him several times during their courtship, Dick knew she was asking for Amy's benefit, but he didn't mind. His voice was full of pride as he said, "The ranch has been in my family for generations. It used to include most of the valley; that's how it got its name, the Sprawling T. But through the years, most of the original ranch has either been sold off or developed, until now the section we have is the largest portion of the original homestead that is still intact. I manage it, but my sisters are co-owners with me."

This was something new to Maggie. "Do they live there too?" she asked.

"Alicia doesn't. Her husband is some kind of junior ambassador, so they move around a lot. Right now, they're living in Washington, D.C., but Helen, my other sister, and her husband John built a house on the ranch." He glanced at Maggie. "Remember, you met Helen the last time you were at the ranch."

"Yes, but I didn't recall that her husband was a rancher."

"He isn't. John made it very clear from the beginning that he prefers the regular hours of running his hardware store. Helen's oldest son is going to be the rancher in the family. He's worked around the ranch since he was old enough to stay on a horse."

Maggie smiled. "Yes, I remember meeting him too. Isn't his name Derek?" She waited for Dick to nod and then continued, "How many children does Helen have? I seem to remember her mentioning some others."

Dick chuckled. "She has six in all."

"Six! My word!" Maggie exclaimed.

In the back seat, Amy's mouth curled downward in dismay. So, not only did she have Lisa to worry about, but there would be six more relatives to contend with.

"Look, Amy." Her mother pointed suddenly. "There's the sign."

Amy looked out of the window just in time to see a large billboard giving directions to the Sprawling T Guest Ranch.

She read the sign quickly and then, not trusting her eyes, asked, "Guest ranch? But I thought . . . ?"

"We have fifteen guest cottages that we rent in the summer, but the main business of the ranch is raising beef cattle. We put up that sign because so many of our guests complained about getting lost looking for us," Dick explained as he turned off Highway 80 onto a narrow, winding, two-lane road.

Amy's spirits lifted immeasurably when she saw the large brick pillars with a crossbar high overhead that marked the entrance to the Sprawling T. It would certainly be easier to get through the summer at a pleasant guest ranch, she thought.

Expecting to see a resortlike atmosphere, Amy was again sharply disappointed. After rounding several more turns, Dick brought the car to a stop in front of a large, rustic building of weathered stone and old wood.

"Look! The moving truck is already here," Maggie said. "At least we won't have to wait to get settled in."

"But why is it parked here?" Amy asked.

"It's our new home. This is the main building of the ranch. There's a reception area and dining room on the ground floor, and we have private living quarters upstairs."

Amy looked at her mother in horror. They were going to live over a hotel lobby!

Maggie sensed Amy's shock and put her arm around her shoulders. "You'll love it. It's big and spacious, and it has a wonderful view of the hills and the rest of the ranch."

Propelled forward by her mother's arm, Amy had no choice but to move woodenly up the steps. Just when she thought she was ready to accept the changes thrust upon her, something else came along! Wouldn't things ever be normal again?

Their steps seemed to echo in the large, cavernous room. Amy was aware of a lot of dark wood paneling and oak beams that exposed the ceiling. At one end of the room was a gigantic fireplace; at the other end there were tables set up for dining. Near the fireplace some couches and chairs had been arranged around a television set, and opposite this lounging area was a reception desk.

"Isn't it wonderful! Can't you just feel its permanence? And look at this fireplace. Won't it be perfect to gather around it in winter? Dick says they have a lot of snow up here. We can have a Christmas tree that reaches to the ceiling." Maggie was as excited as a child at Christmas. "Come on, let me show you our room," she said, leading the way up the stairs to the second floor.

The first room they entered was similar in many ways to the one downstairs. It wasn't quite as large, but it had the same paneling and stone. There were some photographs and curios on the bookshelves that gave it a somewhat more personal atmosphere.

"The master bedroom faces the front of the lodge, and your bedroom looks out toward the mountains. See how large it is," Maggie said hurrying ahead to open the door.

It was definitely a bedroom, but it was already occupied and the furniture in it wasn't hers. "Is this going to be my room?" Amy asked suspiciously.

"Yours and Lisa's."

"You mean I don't even get my own room?" This seemed to be the last straw and tears filled her eyes.

Maggie tried to explain. "Amy, there are only two bedrooms, but there's plenty of room in here. You'll have your own closet and you and Lisa will share a bathroom."

Dick had come in behind them and noticed the pleading tone in Maggie's voice. "Is something wrong?" he asked.

Maggie nodded. "Amy was expecting to have her own room. Being an only child, she's used to having her own private place."

Dick scratched his head. "Yeah, Lisa has too. I guess I didn't think that the girls might want to keep their privacy." He studied the room a minute before saying, "It shouldn't be a major problem to put a partition up and divide this room into two smaller ones if that's what they want."

Maggie beamed and gave him a grateful hug. "See," she said to Amy, "everything will work out."

"I came up here to tell you that the movers are ready to bring up your things if you'll tell them where to put everything," Dick said.

"Oh, good! The sooner we have our own things around us, the sooner we'll feel at home," Maggie said.

"Daddy! Maggie!" A voice called from below and was immediately followed by the sound of rushing footsteps on the stairs. Amy turned curiously toward the door. She was anxious to see the newest member of her family, the girl with whom she would be sharing a room.

Lisa Thompkins entered with the exuberance of someone who had lived all her life in wide-open spaces. She gave quick, warm hugs to her father and Maggie. "Why didn't you tell anyone you were getting married?" she asked.

"We figured that since it was a second marriage for each of us, it would be more appropriate to have a small, simple ceremony without all the fuss," her father explained.

"I hope your feelings weren't hurt," Maggie added.

"Of course not! At least now that you and Dad are married, he'll be staying at home more. I was beginning to feel like an abandoned child." She laughed.

While they greeted each other, Amy was able to get a good look at Lisa. Her shoulder-length, mahogany-colored hair was tied carelessly at the nape of her neck, but it did nothing to detract from her striking face with its high cheekbones, large dark eyes, and wide mouth. Lisa was two or three inches taller than Amy was and her active life had given her a body that was so fit and trim that Amy felt awkward by comparison.

Introductions were unnecessary, so Dick and Maggie tactfully excused themselves to give the girls a chance to get acquainted.

Lisa moved into the room and sat on the side of her bed, leaning back until she rested on her elbows. She studied her new stepsister openly, taking in Amy's soft blond hair and large blue eyes, the delicate pink-and-white complexion. "You don't look like your mother," she stated matter-of-factly.

"Really? Most people say I do."

Lisa shrugged. "Maggie seems more down to earth—the kind of person you can tell your problems to and you know she would understand because she's had problems too."

"Oh? And what do I seem like?" Amy couldn't resist asking, even though she wasn't entirely sure she wanted this cool, outspoken girl to appraise her.

Lisa smiled slightly. "I don't know. A princess, maybe. Someone who's used to having her own way."

Amy's mouth fell open before she could snap it shut. "You couldn't be more wrong," she said. Looking around her, she couldn't help thinking that if she were a princess, then she must be Cinderella, complete with a wicked stepsister!

Lisa caught the look on her face. "You don't like it here, do you?"

Amy decided to be as truthful and blunt as Lisa was. "Until a week ago, I assumed I'd still be living in San Francisco. Now, suddenly, I'm at a ranch somewhere in the mountains, living over a hotel lobby, with a roommate. I guess you could say I'm having a little trouble shifting gears."

Instead of being upset by Amy's outburst, Lisa laughed aloud. "I know what you mean. If Dad had decided to move to San Francisco, he would have had to drag me kicking and screaming the whole way there."

Her entire attitude became friendlier, as though she preferred Amy's honesty to the strained silence between them. "I'm not trying to be rude," she said pushing herself off the bed, "but I promised some guests that I would take them fishing at Star Lake. Besides, I think we need to give you a chance to get used to this place—and us." She flashed Amy another smile. "After all, we'll have plenty of time to get to know each other."

On her way out, Lisa passed Maggie coming in. "Amy," Maggie said, "I thought I'd tell the movers to put your boxes in here, and you can unpack later and decide where you want to put everything."

"That's fine," Amy said listlessly. "But do you need me right now? I think I'd like to take a walk."

"Sure, go ahead," her mother said. "After being cooped up in the car all day, it'll do you good."

Amy made her way to the porch of the lodge and stood there a minute trying to take in everything. Across the road was a large barn surrounded on three sides by a corral where some horses moved about lazily. To the left, she could see two neat rows of cottages and a medium-sized swimming pool. There were no familiar sounds or people. Just Amy and miles and miles of green hills.

Her experience with horses was so limited it was practically nonexistent, but she felt drawn to them; cautiously she began to make her way toward the corral for a closer look when suddenly a voice shouted "Head her back!"

Amy turned just in time to see a horse burst out of the open barn door. Seeing Amy in its path, the horse stopped. But Amy was just as anxious to avoid a confrontation as the horse was, and acting solely on instinct, she ran to the fence and tried to flatten herself against it, burying her face in her hands.

With its path now clear, the horse stretched out and raced across the parking area and down the unpaved road toward the highway.

"Why didn't you do something?" the same voice demanded.

Amy hesitantly turned to face a dark-haired boy about her own age, wearing work-stained jeans. She looked to see if someone had come up behind her, but there was no one else in sight. "Me?" she asked in confusion.

"I don't see anyone else around here, do you?" he asked, frustration and anger written all over his face as he headed toward her.

Just as Amy decided she was in as much danger from him as she had been from the horse, he grasped the top rail of the corral fence and, in a single, fluid motion, hoisted himself over it.

"But I don't know anything about horses," she called to his departing back.

"It doesn't take much education to flap your arms and turn an animal back," he said without looking at her. "Now I'll have to go chase her down heaven knows where! She could be all the way out on the highway by now."

While he was chewing her out, the boy had taken another horse from the group in the corral and brought it to the fence to saddle, his jerky movements giving further evidence of his anger.

It had been a long and difficult day and Amy finally exploded. "I don't know who you are or why you're so upset with me—but I didn't have anything to do with that horse running away. Maybe if you had done a better job of controlling her yourself, you wouldn't have to blame someone else for letting her get away."

Her words brought him up sharply, and for the first time he stopped what he was doing and really looked at her. A frown creased his forehead. "Who are you, anyway?"

She drew herself up proudly. "Amy Longeway, Mr. Thompkins' stepdaughter."

A curious light came to his eyes. "Maggie's daughter?" he asked, and when she nodded, he shrugged. "At least I didn't go shooting my mouth off to one of the guests," was all he offered by way of an apology.

Amy was so shocked, all she could do was stare after him as he mounted his horse and rode off in the same direction the escaped horse had taken.

In spite of her anger, Amy couldn't help admiring the grace and skill with which he rode. She stood staring long after he had disappeared from sight.

2

As soon as he had rounded the first curve, which put him out of sight of the barn, Derek slowed his horse to an easy trot. For some inexplicable reason, he had let that prissy girl goad him into making a big dramatic chase scene when he knew full well he would never catch Daffy by running toward her at a full gallop.

She had too much of a head start for him to catch her on the run. His only hope was that she had stopped before she got to the highway. While he rode, his eyes were constantly searching the landscape for any sign of the runaway horse.

Finally, he spotted her contentedly cropping grass under a tree. Instead of lashing out at her as he really wanted to do, Derek walked his horse as close to her as he dared. Dismounting slowly, he eased toward her, talking in a calm, soothing tone until he was able to get his hand on her bridle.

Working quickly, he attached a lead line and led Daffy back to the barn where she belonged. However, this time, instead of just looping her reins over the top rail of the stall as he had done before, he tied them securely.

Grudgingly, he admitted to himself that he was a little disappointed that Dick's new stepdaughter was no longer around to see how expertly he had managed to bring Daffy back. She'd had no business telling him he couldn't control a horse. He'd trained all the horses in the corral and it wasn't his fault that in spite of her training, Daffy persisted in being unpredictable.

He had grown up dividing his time between chores at home and helping Dick at the ranch. He knew every animal and trail so intimately that although he still had a year of high school to go, the leisure activities of the ranch guests had become primarily his responsibility. When Dick had taken off for the week, Derek had moved into the bunkhouse to be on call in case anyone needed anything at night.

There had been no problems out of the ordinary, but he was glad that Dick was back, for suddenly he felt the need to get away from the ranch and enjoy a little mothering himself. Irritated at Daffy, Amy, and himself, Derek finished bedding down the other horses and went to find his uncle. After filling Dick in on everything that had happened during his absence, Derek started home for the first time in a week.

He had developed a sixth sense that warned him if something wasn't right, and now it nagged at him persistently. It wasn't because he'd had to chase that crazy horse all over creation. In his years of working with animals, this wasn't the first time he had wasted energy in that way and sometimes with less than satisfactory results. It had to do with that girl. Somehow, he just knew she meant trouble.

Usually Derek drove the jeep home, except for occasions such as the present one, when he was working on gentling a horse; then he rode it everywhere and every chance he could, and that included riding it home.

When Derek arrived, one of his younger brothers was in the barn just finishing bedding down their own horses.

Derek called to him as he swung down from the saddle. "Hey, Jason. How about putting Daffy up for me?"

"Sure," Jason said, coming over to take the reins.

Jason had a keen interest in animals and was extremely good with them. Even though the boy was only thirteen, Derek felt more confident in leaving Daffy in Jason's capable hands than he would have in those of fifteen-year-old Matt's. Matt could be a good worker when he wanted to be, but like his father, he had already made it clear that a rancher's life wasn't for him.

"She's already led me on one wild goose chase today, so she's probably tired enough to behave now, but you'd better watch her anyway," Derek said, cautioning his brother before heading to the house.

Derek entered through the washroom, where he stopped to take off his boots and hang his hat on a peg. "Ma, you home?" he called out, listening expectantly for her quick steps.

"Well, hello, stranger," Helen Jansen said as she came to greet him and give him a warm hug. "I was beginning to think you were just a voice over the telephone." She laughed as they made their way into the kitchen. "I take it Dick and Maggie got back today?"

"Yeah, and I guess they were moving in her things. I saw a moving truck pulled up in front of the lodge."

"Good. I'm so glad that Dick has found someone to make a home for him and Lisa. Maggie is just perfect," she said as she handed Derek a cold drink from the refrigerator. "By the way, did you remember to bring your dirty clothes home?"

His look told her he hadn't. "I'm sorry, Ma. I rode that crazy Daffy home, and I just didn't think about them," he said.

"Don't forget them tomorrow, or you're likely to run out of clean clothes to wear," she said and then asked, "By the way, how is Daffy coming along?"

He shrugged. "Darned if I know. She's a comfortable

horse to ride; she has an easy gait and she's very responsive, but she's still too skittish. She'll be doing fine, and then the slightest noise or change in her routine and she just bolts. Runs as though she hasn't got a lick of sense.''

"Have you decided what you're going to do with her?''

He shook his head. "I can't put her in the corral for the guests to ride because I can't trust her. I guess I'll try to work with her a while longer, but if she doesn't settle down soon, we'll have to put her up for sale.''

Helen listened sympathetically, as she did with all her children, and when he had finished his drink, said to him, "Go ahead and have your shower. We'll eat dinner as soon as everyone else gets here.''

In starts and stops, they all finally gathered for dinner. Now that the children were older it was becoming increasingly rare for the whole family to be present for any meal.

During the few minutes of comparative silence at the beginning of the meal, while they were all busy taking the edge off their appetites, Helen asked Derek, "Did you meet Maggie's daughter?''

"I saw her," Derek answered evasively, keeping his eyes on his plate.

When he didn't elaborate, Theresa, his nineteen-year-old sister, asked impatiently, "Well, what's she like?''

He shrugged. "A girl."

"That doesn't tell us anything," Theresa said complainingly. "Stacy and I"—she nodded toward their eleven-year-old sister—"are both girls, but we aren't anything alike.''

"I don't know," Derek said, searching his mind for details. He knew full well that his sister wouldn't be satisfied until he told them something specific. "She's about Lisa's age, kind of small, and has blond hair and a temper.''

"I'll bet she's pretty," Matt said; he had just begun to be interested in girls.

Derek eyed his brother sharply. "Why do you say that?''

"'Cause you looked funny when you talked about her,'' Matt answered, smirking.

"I'll bet she's an angel,'' Adam, the youngest member of the family, chimed in. His favorite book was one of Bible stories that had a picture of an angel looking down at the baby Jesus. Adam had been so impressed with the picture of the blond, blue-eyed angel that he had insisted on giving everything that name. They already had a horse, a dog, and a chicken named Angel, and no one doubted that if Helen had another child, it would be named that also.

Derek almost choked on his food. "She's no angel. I'm sure of that!'' he said emphatically. "Now can we drop the subject?''

To his relief, they did.

Derek had declared that Amy wasn't an angel, and at that moment she would have had to agree with him, because she found her present situation far from heavenly. Trying to forget her troubles by staying busy, she had thrown herself into the job of unpacking.

With the help of the movers, she had set up her bed on the opposite side of the room from Lisa's, and she had hung her clothes in the empty closet or put them away in her chest. All she still had ahead of her were the boxes of personal items that crowded the room.

"How are you doing?'' her mother asked, threading her way through the maze of boxes.

"All right, I guess,'' Amy answered, gesturing to what she'd already accomplished. "I'm going to need a small table of some kind to set up my stereo and records.''

"That's no problem. With all the duplications between our furniture and Dick's, we must have something you can use,'' Maggie said, sitting down on the side of the bed. "But that's not really what I meant. I was trying to ask you how you felt.''

Amy was sitting cross-legged on the floor, and instead of looking at her mother, she stared at the floor. "I don't know. Maybe I'm still in shock.'' Reluctantly, she met her mother's eyes. ''Why didn't you tell me you were planning to get married and move up here?''

''There really wasn't time. Dick and I had decided to get married, but we hadn't even started thinking about setting a date. Then, when he came to see me last weekend, and we started talking about how busy he was at the ranch all summer and that he wouldn't be able to get away to see me very often, we just decided to go ahead and get married right away and work out all the problems together.''

''But what about my problems? You weren't the only one with a life in San Francisco. I had my friends and my plans. I was just appointed to the school yearbook staff for next year, and I was supposed to be secretary for the Drama Club.'' Knowing that her mother hadn't been one of Stephen Kemp's admirers, Amy didn't mention that she had also left him.

''Dick told me that he gave you a choice of going back there for the school year or staying here,'' Maggie said hesitantly.

''Are you going to let me?'' Amy's heart stopped beating as she waited for her mother to answer.

''Is that really what you want to do?''

Amy raised up on her knees to grasp her mother's. ''Mom, it's not a question of choosing between you and my friends back there, but I have thought about it, and yes—I could be happy in San Francisco as long as I knew you were happy and being taken care of here.''

Impulsively, Maggie gave her a hug. ''You really are thoughtful, and I know you care.''

''Then I can go back?''

''Well, Dick also told me that he had given you some provisions, so I think I'll leave it entirely up to you and him,'' she answered. ''But let's not worry about that yet. It's time for dinner, so why don't you clean up a bit and come on down?''

Amy had been so busy, she hadn't even thought about eating, but once she saw all the tempting food spread out on the buffet table, she realized that she was hungry.

There were several other groups of people sitting at individual tables, eating and talking amiably. "Who are they?" Amy asked when she joined her mother, Dick, and Lisa at their table.

"They're some of our guests," Dick answered. "Even though it's still pretty early in the season, we've already rented six cabins."

"Do you ever rent all of them?" Maggie asked.

"Oh yes, by the last week of July we have to turn people away," Dick said. "We've thought about putting up some more cottages, but we really can't handle any more guests. As it is, they keep us pretty busy."

Before Amy could wonder if that would include her, her mother indicated that it would. "Well, now you have four more hands. What can Amy and I do?"

Lisa grinned. "Take your pick. There are cabins to be cleaned and meals to cook. Someone has to be at the registration desk all the time, and we have to take care of the livestock and take guests on trail rides or fishing. The list goes on and on."

"What do you do?" Maggie asked Lisa.

"Some of all of it, except cooking, of course. We do have someone who takes care of that. And there are two local ladies who come in every day during the summer to clean the cabins, but when we're crowded, they need help. Derek, my cousin, usually takes care of the horses, but when some of the guests want to go on trail rides and others want to do something else, I help him out."

"I can help clean the cabins," Maggie said.

Amy felt they expected her to volunteer to do something, so she said, "Is it very difficult to watch the desk? Maybe I could do that?"

"The hardest part of that job is sitting around inside

when there's nothing to do,'' Lisa assured her. "But someone has to be there to work the switchboard, take reservations, and deliver messages.''

"Amy won't want to spend all of her summer indoors,'' Dick said.

"I can relieve her,'' Maggie suggested.

"Me too,'' Lisa said.

For the remainder of the meal, they discussed the ranch and recalled anecdotes from previous years until Lisa asked, "Dad, may I go to a movie tonight with the Hastys? You know I didn't leave the ranch a single time the whole week you were gone.''

Dick smiled. "Since you have been so responsible, I don't see why not, but I think it would be nice of you to invite Amy to go with you.''

"That's not necessary,'' Amy spoke up quickly.

"It's not a date or anything. I'm just going with Barbara and Robbie Hasty. They're just friends,'' Lisa said.

"I think I'd better stay and finish unpacking,'' Amy said, and then, to show Dick that she wasn't trying to be difficult, added, "but thanks for asking me.''

"Sure, suit yourself,'' Lisa said indifferently. "I'm going to run up and shower and change before they get here.''

Amy busied herself becoming familiar with the downstairs area of the lodge until Lisa left and she was sure she'd be alone in the room. Maybe it was silly, but she didn't want anyone else around while she sorted through her personal things.

When she opened the first box, she was assailed by a wave of homesickness. Her stuffed-animal collection and pastel water colors looked so strange in this stark room, as if they, like she, didn't belong here. Doggedly, Amy kept at her job until all the boxes except one were empty.

The last box contained her souvenirs—the scrapbooks, class pictures, crushed napkins, old notes and letters, and faded ribbons that proved she had existed in another place and were tokens of the happy times she had had there. Carefully, almost reverently, she lifted out each item and examined it, reliving the old days. She picked up an envelope of loose snapshots from the bottom, and the pictures scattered on the floor beside her.

"Darn," she muttered as she collected the photos. Most of them were of her and Shannon Grady, her best friend. Shannon had transferred to Bay View High School the same year that Amy had, and the two girls had immediately formed a fast friendship based on common fears, needs, and interests in such things as music, fashion, and boys—like Stephen Kemp.

Amy, Shannon, and the entire female half of the student body could pinpoint the exact day that he transferred to their school. It was more than just his blond good looks, though they were spectacular enough; he had a special aura about him that set him apart. Unlike the other transfer students, Stephen didn't stand meekly on the fringes of the main body of students waiting to be asked to join something or trying to find a place in the crowd. He forged ahead and created his own place. Within a month, he had organized a rock band and was playing at all the important parties and eventually at some of the school functions. His first year there, he was chosen captain of the tennis and the debating teams.

Amy's circle of friends had even invented a game, with the unsuspecting Stephen as the playing piece. If one of them saw him, she got one point; a lucky girl could get five points for speaking to him and ten for engaging him in private conversation. The first girl who was fortunate enough to get a date with him was to be declared the winner.

But Amy had soon tired of the childish game and decided to play for keeps. With the same thoroughness with which she prepared for any exam, she began studying Stephen. She researched all of his likes and dislikes. She even attended some of his debates and jotted down the important points he made. She learned that he was bored with

professional football and with studying energy conserva-
tion, but that he was interested in soccer, local politics, and
saving San Francisco's endangered cable cars.

When she felt fully prepared, Amy put her plan into
action by organizing a group of students to contribute to the
restoration of the cable cars. Their first project was to hold a
dance and donate all the proceeds to that worthy cause. Of
course, it was just a "lucky" accident that she asked
Stephen's band to play for the dance.

After she had his attention, the really hard job of keeping
it began. Since he had almost every girl in school worship-
ping at his feet, Amy decided to be different and present
him with a challenge.

And it had worked! He had even actually asked her to go
steady. More than anything, she had wanted to accept, but
in spite all of her pleading, and Shannon's support, her
mother had adamantly refused to allow her to go steady at
barely sixteen.

"If you still feel the same way next year, we can discuss
it then," was all her mother would say.

Naturally, Amy hadn't told any of this to Stephen. She
had preferred to let him believe that it was she who didn't
want to be tied down, when in truth, she had worried
constantly that he would get tired of playing this waiting
game and move on to someone else.

Amy had saved Stephen's pictures to unpack last, and
now she took them out and propped them up around her.
There was an eight-by-ten class picture that he had given
her and some snapshots that she had taken of him on the
tennis courts, at debates, and with his band. She relived
their last date as she stared at the pictures that didn't really
do justice to his incredible smoky gray eyes and the golden
highlights in his hair.

They had planned to go to the movies, but Stephen's
band practice had lasted so long, they had just gone out for
pizza instead. There in the semiprivacy of a back booth,

surrounded by the tangy smell of tomato sauce and oregano, she had told him she was moving.

"Where? When did this happen?"

"This week. Mom just called from Nevada. She and Mr. Thompkins eloped. They'll be home in a few days, and then we're moving to his ranch in the Sierra Nevadas. The movers are already packing our things."

He had reached across the table and had taken her hands in his. "You poor kid," he murmured as he lowered his head and brought her fingers to meet his lips. "Does that mean I won't see you anymore?"

Amy would have preferred a more emphatic declaration, something like, "They'll never separate us!" but she accepted what he offered. "I'll be back from time to time to visit my grandmother. I can see you then."

"But it's not going to be the same. I'll really miss you, Amy. I've never met anyone like you."

"We could write to each other," she suggested hopefully.

"I guess so, but a letter's not the same as having someone with you," he had said.

But now, she thought as she hugged her knees, maybe there wouldn't be any need to write many letters—just enough to keep him from forgetting her until she got back. By then she would be old enough to go steady, and somehow she'd get him to ask her again. After all, she had done it once.

But that would have to wait until September. Between now and then, she had to convince Dick that she was the most cooperative and mature teenager he had ever known.

With renewed enthusiasm, she finished putting away her things, and after taking the boxes outside to be carted away, she went in to take a long, relaxing bath.

She was putting on her pajamas when she heard Lisa come in downstairs. Quickly, she flipped off the lights and jumped into bed. With a great effort she forced herself to slow her breathing until it was coming in the soft even breaths of someone fast asleep.

Lying there in the semidarkness, listening to Lisa get ready for bed, she couldn't help thinking how strange it was to be sharing a bedroom after all these years. Mentally, she prepared herself for a long night of waiting for sleep to come, but almost before she knew it, the sun was tickling her eyelids.

3

Amy rolled over onto her stomach and tried hiding her head under her arms to block out the sun so she could go back to sleep, but her body was well rested and demanded action.

With a sigh of resignation, she climbed quietly out of bed so as not to disturb Lisa, who was snoring softly on her side of the room. Amy dressed in a pair of old, well-worn jeans and a warm sweatshirt and made her way downstairs.

She could hear someone moving around and followed the sound to the front desk, where she found Dick nursing a cup of coffee and going over the registration book.

"Good morning." He smiled in greeting. "You're up early."

Amy returned a sheepish smile. "I forgot to close my curtains last night and the sun woke me up."

The door to the kitchen opened, and the husband-and-wife team that Amy had seen serving dinner the night before came in to begin setting up the breakfast buffet. Dick introduced them as Fred and Mary Avery.

"My, aren't you a pretty little thing!" Fred said. "How old are you?"

"Sixteen."

He shook his head. "I declare, sixteen gets younger-looking every day."

"That's because you keep getting older," his wife said, poking him in the ribs before she turned to Amy. "Come with me, and I'll show you around the kitchen. That way, you'll be able to find anything you need if I'm not around."

Amy followed the older woman into the large, efficient-looking kitchen.

"You can always take anything you want to out of this refrigerator," Mary said, pointing to one of three refrigerators lined against the wall. "And I keep snacks and baked goods in the first cabinet by the door. We serve three meals in the dining room every day, but we don't have room service. Each cabin has a small stove and refrigerator in case the guests want to fix something in their rooms."

As she explained the procedure, Mary went about breaking a dozen eggs into a large bowl. Amy was so fascinated watching her work, she caught only half of what Mary was saying.

Mary stirred the eggs and then began separating a pound of bacon to put on the grill. "You can get the orange juice out of the second fridge and fill up some glasses," she told Amy.

When Amy returned to the dining room with the juice, she found that Dick had been joined by three guys in the rough clothes of ranch hands with western hats and boots.

"Amy, come here." Dick called. "I want you to meet some more of the family."

Though inwardly she was still chafing over the sudden move and the loss of her friends and Stephen, Amy wasn't so depressed that she couldn't appreciate the healthy good looks of the younger men.

On closer observation, as Dick introduced James and

Ricky Williams, his younger cousins, and Derek Jansen, his nephew, only James could be classified as a man. He had the slightly thickened body that maturity brings, and he wore a wedding ring. Ricky, his brother, while not quite an adult, smiled at her in the faintly patronizing manner of someone past the age of being seriously interested in a high school kid. She instantly recognized Derek as the boy she had run into at the corral the day before.

"Dick, your marriage has certainly brought some welcome changes around here," Ricky said teasingly. "I definitely approve."

Under his appraisal of her, Amy could feel her face growing warm. Ricky noticed the rise in her color and pointed it out delightedly. "Look, she even blushes!"

He threw his arm around Amy's shoulders in a natural, friendly manner, as if he had known her for years. "Lord, I love a girl who blushes!" he said effusively.

"And girls who giggle, or pout, or cry. . . . ," James added dryly.

Ricky took a good-natured swipe at his brother. "You're just jealous 'cause you're married now and aren't free to flirt with pretty girls anymore," he said with a broad wink at Amy.

Under the cover of their horseplay, Amy glanced at Derek to see his reaction to the attention that Ricky and James were paying her, but he seemed totally unaware of it. His eyes had contained only a flicker of recognition when Dick introduced them and while Ricky and James were taking the time to make her feel welcome, Derek went to the buffet to get his breakfast.

She dismissed his aloof behavior with a shrug and made her own way to the buffet. She was more interested in the light-hearted banter from Ricky than she was in food, and she followed him to the table where Dick, James, and Derek were already seated.

"How many more cows are due to calve soon?" Dick directed his question at James.

"Three more calved yesterday. That leaves about seven that should have their calves within a week."

"Keep a close eye on them. I want the whole herd moved to the summer pasture just as soon as possible. We need to start getting this one ready for their winter feed."

Amy considered the possibilities of working beside Ricky and found the idea very intriguing. "What do you do at the ranch? Do you help with the guests?" she asked him.

Ricky flashed his ready grin. "No. Dick makes me stay out in the pasture taking care of the livestock and mending fences. Personally, I think he's afraid to let me spend too much time around all the pretty girls who come here."

"The truth of the matter is that you'd spend all your time flirting instead of getting any work done," Derek said.

"I think the guests would appreciate having someone charming around," Amy said in Ricky's behalf.

"See, cuz," Ricky said with an appreciative chuckle, "that's what I've been trying to tell you. You oughta let me give you some lessons."

"I don't need to know anything that you could teach me," Derek said flatly.

"That's debatable," Amy said under her breath.

Her voice was so low it was lost on everyone except Derek, whose unreadable expression gave no clue that he had heard.

Dick had finished his breakfast, and as he stood up to leave he said, "Since Amy's up before anyone else this morning, why don't you take her for a little tour of the place?"

"I'd be glad to," Ricky volunteered.

"No. I want you to go with James and check on the fences of the summer pasture while he checks on the cows. I meant Derek."

To Amy, Derek's reply seemed less enthusiastic. There was a slight pause before he said, "Sure, if she can be ready to go in a few minutes. I have a trail ride scheduled for this morning."

Irritated that he spoke about her, rather than to her, Amy stood up abruptly. "I'm ready now."

"Fine," Derek said. Without waiting to see whether she was following him, he got up and headed for the door, grabbing his hat and jacket off the rack as he went by it.

Even though it was early summer, it was a cold morning, and Amy's sweatshirt, which had been adequate inside the lodge, was less than that now. But she was determined that she would freeze to death before she asked him to wait for her to go get a jacket.

To take her mind off the cold, Amy focused her attention on Derek as he strode purposefully in front of her. He wasn't particularly big or imposing by sheer size, but there was something about the way he carried himself that said he was a person to be reckoned with. His skin seemed to be stretched tautly over a framework of muscles that were so tightly coiled they gave a spring to his walk. His dark hair was almost completely hidden by his hat, and even though his back was to Amy, she could recall with clarity the startling blueness of his eyes, surrounded by dark brows and lashes.

"You want to pick out a mount?" Derek called to her over his shoulder.

Amy, not yet used to the high altitude and slightly breathless from the cold, was having some difficulty keeping up with him. "You mean a horse? I can't ride."

Her words brought him up sharply as he pivoted to a stop. "You can't ride a horse?"

"No, I can't. Believe it or not, they wouldn't let us keep horses in our fourth-floor apartment."

"Then we'll have to take the jeep. That might be better anyway. At least it'll be faster."

His words brought hot color back into Amy's cheeks. "By all means. I'd hate for this to take any longer than necessary."

Derek had the decency to look embarrassed. "I didn't mean it that way. It's just that there's a lot of territory to cover—and remember, I do have a trail ride that has to go out on time.''

Reluctantly, Amy followed him to the jeep and climbed in beside him, her teeth tightly clenched to keep them from chattering.

Derek shrugged out of his jacket and, without a word, handed it to her.

"No, thanks, I don't need it." Amy said through stiff lips.

"Of course you don't," he said. "I suppose you always go around with blue lips."

It was bad enough that Dick expected him to be her baby-sitter, he thought; but the least she could do was to be halfway pleasant. She'd managed that pretty well at breakfast with Ricky and James making a fuss over her.

Their eyes met in a silent war of wills until Amy, sensing the greater determination in Derek, combined with the fact that she really was cold, took the jacket from him and admitted defeat by forgetting to stifle the sigh of contentment as she burrowed into the jacket's deep pile lining. She was immediately surrounded by an unfamiliar, though not unpleasant, scent of horses, fresh hay, and the spicy masculine aroma of his aftershave lotion.

Derek gunned the jeep but didn't move his foot toward the accelerator. Instead, he turned his head to one side and looked at Amy. She had snuggled so far down in his jacket that only her nose and big blue eyes were visible. He swallowed the grin that had started to form. "Listen, we seemed to have gotten off on the wrong foot. I don't know what I've done, but . . ."

Amy's eyes widened in surprise. "You don't remember yelling at me yesterday?"

Derek's eyes clouded in thought and then he said slowly, "Yeah, but it didn't mean anything. I do that to everybody. Besides, if I remember the incident correctly, you yelled back."

"What did you expect? I don't know what anybody else

does when you treat them as you did me—but I won't stand for it!''

"Is this a declaration of war?"

"It doesn't have to be. That's strictly up to you."

"Well, I hope you don't expect me to flirt with you like Ricky does."

"No, but I think even you should be able to manage being civil."

"I'll try," he said curtly as he applied pressure to the gas pedal and put the jeep in motion.

In the bored tone of a hired guide who wasn't particularly enjoying his job, Derek began identifying the various buildings. "The big house is called the lodge, and that"— he pointed across the road—"is the 'big' barn and the corral. We have other barns on the ranch, but they're identified by their specific use—like the hay barn, the calf barn, and so forth." In spite of his irritation, his voice became more animated as he talked about the ranch.

He drove completely around the lodge, giving Amy a closeup view of the swimming pool and the guest cabins. The jeep picked up speed as they left the building complex behind and began to climb a steep grade that led into the mountains. "Have you ever spent much time out in the country before?" Derek asked over the noise of the engine.

Amy shook her head.

"You'll love it. There's no better place in the whole world to live," he said emphatically.

Amy grimaced. "So I've been told."

"But you don't agree?"

"I think it depends on the person. Some of us prefer being surrounded by interesting people, city lights, theaters, museums, and shops."

"What about the pollution, crime, and traffic jams?"

Amy sighed in exasperation. "I didn't say that living in a city didn't have drawbacks, but then you can't honestly claim that life on a ranch is perfect either."

"No, but it's a lot better than any city I've been in."

She couldn't resist the impulse to put him down. "Oh? And how many cities have you visited?"

"Quite a few, actually," Derek said. "I've visited Aunt Alicia in Washington, D.C., and one summer I went with her to Europe. When I was younger, I use to stay with my grandparents every summer in San Jose, but I could never wait to get back here."

Derek guided the jeep around a sharp curve and brought it to a stop. "From up there"—he pointed to a large boulder that jutted out from the side of the mountain—"you can get a good view of practically the whole ranch," he said, getting out of the jeep and leading the way.

Up close, Amy could see that the rock plateaued about five or six feet above her head. One side of it had crude steps that made it possible, if not exactly easy, to climb. Derek scampered up to the top and then turned to give her a hand as she struggled up behind him.

They hadn't driven very long, but because the entire route had been uphill, the ranch buildings below them now looked like a scene done in miniature. The white caps of snow on the surrounding mountains contrasted with the deep green of the trees. The ranch that nestled at the foot looked like a picture on a postcard.

Derek stood waiting expectantly until Amy finally managed to say, "It's very nice."

He had seen the view many times, in all seasons, and it never failed to touch some deep responsive chord in him. Now he turned to her in exasperation. "Why are you so determined not to like this place?"

Amy shrugged indifferently. "It's not a question of whether I like it or not. I made an agreement with Dick. If I came here for the summer and didn't complain, he would let me go back to San Francisco in the fall. And that is precisely what I am going to do."

"So that's it! I knew there must be some reason why you had already made up your mind against it."

He studied her face carefully, taking in the tousled blond

hair that was pushed up around her ears by the collar of his coat and the rosy glow the wind had brought to her cheeks, and felt a crazy lurch in the pit of his stomach. Roughly, he pushed aside his uncomfortable thoughts and said more harshly than necessary, "What is it? Are you afraid that you might actually start to like it here and not want to go back?"

"No, that isn't it at all," she insisted angrily. "But if this is the end of the tour, could you take me back to the lodge? I think I've seen enough for one day."

Lisa met them as they drove back in. "Where did you two go off to? I thought I was going to have to take the trail ride out by myself."

"Dick asked me to show Amy around," Derek answered for both of them and reached out to ruffle Lisa's hair as he had itched to do to Amy's. "And I didn't forget about the ride. Where is everyone?"

"They're still at breakfast, but we need nine horses, not counting our own."

"Okay, you get the horses and bring them to the fence. I'll go get the tack."

As Lisa and Derek began preparing for the trail ride, Amy was forgotten and without a word to them, she went back to the lodge where she found her mother and Dick at the desk.

Maggie looked up with a smile. "Did you enjoy the tour?"

Amy forced a matching smile. "Oh, yes." She had been so comfortable in Derek's jacket that she had forgotten she had it on until the warmth of the lodge made her uncomfortable. Instead of going back to return it, she just slipped it off and hung it on the coat rack beside the desk. "But it was colder than I imagined," she said, explaining the jacket.

"Come over here while Dick explains what we need to know about the front desk," Maggie said. "It's not as complicated as it looks."

Her mother was right. In a large registration book, each

rented cabin had a separate column where all the charges for each day were recorded, and an appointment book listed the dates and cabins already reserved. Even the switchboard, though it looked antiquated, didn't have a lot of complicated switches, and the hookups to each cabin were clearly numbered.

After Dick had gone over everything twice, Maggie asked, "Could you watch the desk while I go out and help clean the cabins?"

"I think so," Amy said with more confidence than she felt. But watching the desk was preferable to doing any outside chores, and she certainly didn't want to help her mother work as a maid!

"If you run into a problem or have to leave the desk for anything, Mrs. Avery is right there in the kitchen," Dick reminded her as he left with Maggie.

Amy watched them go and shook her head. A month ago, her mother would have panicked if she had so much as developed a hangnail, but after one day at this place she was perfectly happy to be cleaning up after paying guests. Well, her mother could live here if she wanted to, Amy thought, but all she wanted to do was just get through the summer—beginning with the first day.

Lisa didn't return from the trail ride until noon, and by then Amy had gotten over most of her nervousness about working behind the desk and was cheerfully honest when Lisa asked how things were going.

"All right, I guess. I had one call for a reservation. Do you want to check to see if I wrote it up correctly?"

Lisa glanced over the book and smiled. "Oh, the Hardys. They come every year and always take the same cabin. I'm glad they didn't skip this year."

"Why? I mean, do you need the money?" Amy asked, thinking that she could see the need for repairs and redecorating.

"It's not that, exactly. They're just special people," Lisa

answered enigmatically and changed the subject. "By the way, have you heard anything from the Jacksons? They're supposed to check in today."

Amy felt a sudden panic that she might have missed a party of guests. "When were they supposed to be here?"

"No specific time," Lisa said reassuringly and dropped the subject. "If you're tired of minding the desk, I'll relieve you whenever you want me to."

"I'm all right for now. Why don't you go ahead and have lunch first?"

"Okay. I'll fix a plate and eat upstairs. When I come down, I'll take over the desk for the afternoon and you can have a break."

Amy looked up as the door opened again, but this time it was only Derek. As if by mutual consent, they both quickly averted their eyes, making any greeting unnecessary. Amy kept her head down, pretending to be studying the registration book, until she heard the kitchen door open and close.

When she heard a door open again, she assumed it was Derek returning and didn't bother to look up until she heard a strange voice say, "We finally made it!"

Startled, Amy jerked her head up and saw a family of four standing in the doorway smiling expectantly at her. Embarrassed at having ignored their entrance, she tried to make up for it with her most charming smile. "You must be the Jacksons."

"No one else," the man answered good-naturedly. "And this is my wife and our two kids, Frank and Laura."

Amy's smile included Mrs. Jackson and the two teenagers. "Welcome to the Sprawling T," she said as she handed Mr. Jackson a registration card.

While he filled out the card, Mr. Jackson commented, "We've been coming here for years, but I've never seen you around before. Don't tell me Dick has finally started hiring some more employees? I was under the impression that he was dead set against making any changes."

"Well, he's made some. He married my mother and sort of got me in the bargain. I'm Amy Longeway."

"Miss Longeway," he said, returning the card and accepting the keys to his cabin, "I think he made a pretty good bargain."

"Thank you. Do you need any help finding your cabin or getting your luggage?"

"No, we'll be fine. We know our way around," Mr. Jackson assured her.

The Jacksons left to get settled in their cabin, and Amy turned to file their registration card, only to be interrupted again.

"Excuse me," Frank Jackson said. He was leaning against the desk, obviously in no hurry to join his family.

"Yes?"

"I just thought I'd ask—I mean, if you're the owner's stepdaughter, surely you don't have to stay behind that desk all the time?"

Amy had been so concerned about registering his family without making any mistakes that she hadn't paid any attention to Frank Jackson. He was a good-looking boy about her own age, with black hair and dark eyes. Amy couldn't help admiring the trim fit of his crisp, new western jeans and the cowboy hat that was pushed back on his head at a rakish angle.

She smiled slowly. "I'm not chained back here, if that's what you mean."

"What about dinner tonight?"

"What about it?" Amy asked, deliberately misunderstanding.

Now Frank smiled, simultaneously lowering his eyelids until his eyes were only narrow slits. It struck Amy that he could have looked incredibly sexy if it hadn't been such an obviously practiced mannerism.

"You're not going to make this easy for me, are you?" he asked.

"It might help if I knew what you were doing," Amy countered.

"I'm trying to ask you to have dinner with me tonight."

Except for her brief encounter with Ricky that morning, this was the most pleasant diversion of the day, and Amy's smile softened. "I'd love to," she said.

"Great! I'll meet you here around seven tonight, then, if that's all right."

They were interrupted by another guest, who called, "Oh, miss?"

Amy nodded to Frank and then turned to the woman, whom she had seen in the dining room earlier. "Yes, may I help you?"

"I hope so. I wanted to go to the swimming pool, but I'm expecting a telephone call from my daughter. Can you transfer it to me out there?"

Amy looked at the switchboard but didn't see an extension for the pool. "I'm sorry. There's no telephone out there, but I could come and get you when your call comes in."

"Oh, thank you. I'd really appreciate that," the woman said. "I'm Mrs. Mary Copeland, in cabin six."

Amy took a sheet of note paper and was tagging the extension for Mrs. Copeland's cabin when Derek's voice came from beside her.

"You handled that well."

The smile on Amy's face froze as she detected the note of surprise in his voice. "You mean, *considering,* don't you?" she said, mocking him.

Derek put both hands on the desk and stared at her crossly. "What's the matter with you? Why can't you just accept the compliment?"

"Not when it comes out sounding like an insult."

"An insult!" he said, his voice growing louder. "Listen, if I'd wanted to insult you, I would have pointed out that it isn't necessary for you to flirt with every boy who comes through the door.''

Realizing that he must have overheard her conversation with Frank Jackson, Amy said, "You're just so bad-tempered, you think anyone who's being friendly is flirting.''

"Derek, there you are!" a sweet, feminine voice called, and Derek and Amy turned to see Laura Jackson hurrying toward them. "I was at the corral looking for you.''

Laura didn't stop until she was inches away from Derek, the scent of her freshly applied cologne more cloying than her voice. "Would you be an angel and take me horseback riding? I don't think I'm good enough to ride with a group yet.''

"But I thought you came here every summer?" Amy asked.

"I do, but I guess I'm not very athletic. I still need some of Derek's expert advice," Laura said, reaching out to touch Derek's arm. "You will help me again this summer, won't you?''

Derek stepped back to avoid her hand but answered politely enough, "I'd be happy to. Why don't you go change into some riding clothes and I'll meet you at the corral in, say, fifteen minutes?''

Amy waited until Laura was out of the lodge before asking, "Now what was it you were saying about not flirting with the guests?''

Derek's temper flared. "You know good and well that I . . .''

"Amy," Lisa called from the stairs, "you can take your break now. I'll take over the desk.''

Derek glanced at his cousin and stopped abruptly. Frustrated, he turned to go and then saw his jacket on the rack where Amy had left it earlier. He grabbed it with such vengeance that the whole rack threatened to topple over and stomped out of the lodge, slamming the door behind him.

Lisa stared after him in amazement. "What on earth is the matter with Derek?"

Amy swallowed, trying to control the laughter in her voice. "I haven't the slightest idea," she said innocently. She exchanged places with Lisa and escaped up the stairs to her room.

4

Amy knew exactly how she was going to spend her break. She was going to write to Stephen. After all, he still didn't know she would be returning to San Francisco in the fall.

Of course, it could be very romantic just to show up in September and surprise him, but she was too insecure to do that. There was nothing she could do to keep him from dating other girls while she was away, but maybe just knowing she would be returning would keep him from becoming too involved with anyone else.

She made herself comfortable in the middle of her bed and worried the tip of her pen as she considered how to begin. Before she had written the first word, the sound of the telephone interrupted her thoughts. Amy went to answer it.

"Amy," Lisa's voice came over the line, "you have a long-distance call. Hold on and I'll put it through."

Amy had only a second to anticipate who would be calling her before she heard Shannon's voice. "I couldn't wait for a letter. What is it like?"

Amy laughed happily. "I can't believe you're calling me so soon."

"We can't talk for hours the way we used to," Shannon warned her. "Mom's already given me a lecture on long-distance rates, so let's not waste time on trivial stuff. Have you met any cute boys yet?"

"Naturally," Amy said, teasing her friend. "This place is just crawling with them. I didn't know until I got here yesterday that this isn't just a working ranch; it's a guest ranch too."

"You lucky stiff!" Shannon complained in mock anger. "Not only do you catch the cutest boy in San Francisco, but now you're branching out to include cowboys."

"The summer is shaping up much better than I thought it would," Amy admitted. "But tell me what's going on there. I feel as if I've been away for a year instead of just a day."

"There's nothing really. Of course, you already know Jeannette's birthday party is tonight, and I guess everyone who hasn't already left for vacation will be there." Shannon paused. "Do you know if Stephen's going to the party?"

Amy stiffened at the mention of Stephen's name. "No. We didn't discuss Jeannette's party on our last date."

Shannon caught the pathos of the "last date" remark. "No, I guess you wouldn't have. I'll keep an eye open for him, and if he comes and looks as though he needs someone to console him, I'll make sure none of the other girls get too close," she said. "Do you want me to tell him anything for you?"

This was the perfect opportunity to tell Shannon that she was planning to come back in the fall, but Amy hesitated. She and Shannon had shared clothes, secrets, and their views on boys, but they had always scrupulously avoided each other's boyfriends. There shouldn't be any reason for her not to trust Shannon now, but Stephen might be too much of a temptation for even her best friend to resist. Besides, her relationship with Stephen was so tenuous that it had to be handled carefully. She wanted to be the one to tell him that she was coming back, and as disloyal as it might seem, Shannon was much too pretty to act as a go-between.

"No . . . not really," Amy finally said. "You can tell him I said hello if he asks."

"Sure, I'd be happy to," Shannon said. "I've got to get off the phone before Mother starts breathing fire, so write me and send me your new address. I'm going to expect at least one letter every week."

When the telephone went dead in her hands, Amy felt more alone and isolated than she had before. If she were at home now, she and Shannon would be coordinating their outfits for Jeannette's party. They would probably agree to meet at the tennis club and then spend more time gossiping at the snack bar than actually playing tennis.

With an effort, Amy shook off the depression that threatened to overwhelm her. After all, she didn't have time to wallow in self-pity if she intended to get on with her plan to keep herself firmly etched in Stephen's mind.

She had already changed her mind about writing him a long letter. It was only two days since she had last seen him, and a long, sentimental letter might show him just how much she cared. What she needed instead was a short, cheery note, and the postcards she had found at the desk would be perfect.

She had chosen one with an aerial view of the ranch that was similar to the view that Derek had shown her earlier that morning. On the back of the card, in small print, was written a brief description: "The Sprawling T Guest Ranch near Truckee, California, is known for its beautiful scenery and rustic atmosphere."

Beneath the descriptive blurb, she wrote:

Dear Stephen,

Greetings from my new summer home in the wilds of California. It is gorgeous here, but after a summer of roughing it, I'll be glad to get back to San Francisco. See you when school starts!

For a minute, she debated on how to sign it, and then in bold script, she wrote, "Love, Amy."

The next move would be up to Stephen. He would either ignore her hint that she would be coming back in September, or he would call or write to find out more.

Please, she prayed, let him care enough to ask.

With a heart full of hope, she took the postcard downstairs to find a mailbox.

"Sure," Lisa said in answer to her question. "It's right at the corner of the fence where you turn to go into the parking area."

"You mean, all the way out by the highway?"

Lisa laughed. "No, not that far. It's right . . . wait a minute. I'll let Mrs. Avery know I'm going to be away from the desk, and I'll walk you out there. It won't take very long."

On their way to the mailbox, Lisa asked, "Would you like to go riding later? There's still a lot of the ranch that you haven't seen."

Amy hesitated. She knew Lisa would find out eventually, so she might as well tell her and get it over with. "I don't know how."

"That's no problem. We have plenty of gentle horses, and any of us could teach you."

"Thanks. Maybe later," Amy said evasively.

After dropping the postcard in the mailbox, they started back toward the lodge and saw Ricky riding up to the barn on a big bay horse. Amy thought he looked incredibly handsome.

As soon as he saw the girls, Ricky swept off his hat in a

grand gesture and, against his horse's wishes, changed his direction to coincide with the girls'.

Ricky smiled at Amy and directed a question at Lisa. "I thought you were going to bring Amy out to the pasture to see the new calves."

Squinting up at him, Lisa explained, "She doesn't ride."

Amy was nervous about the way Ricky kept edging his horse closer and closer to them and was relieved when he swung down from the saddle and fell into step with them.

"I'll teach you," he said. "There's nothing to it."

Before Amy could come up with a suitable excuse, Lisa interrupted. "Isn't it a little early for you to be coming in from the pasture?"

He grinned and tipped his hat. "Yes, boss lady, but your daddy gave me the rest of the week off. Ellen and her family are coming up to Lake Tahoe this week, and I'm going over to spend some time with them. I was just bringing my horse to the barn for Derek to look after while I'm gone."

He finished his explanation and turned back to Amy. "I'll get back to you about those lessons next week," he promised. Without waiting for her to reply, he nodded to the girls and led his horse toward the corral.

"Is Ellen his girl friend?" Amy asked when she was sure Ricky was out of hearing range.

Lisa shrugged. "Ricky changes girl friends so often, it's hard to tell. I think Ellen is some girl he met at college, but I've never bothered to learn much about her. Next week he'll probably have another one anyway."

While she was talking, Lisa continued to watch Ricky until he disappeared inside the barn. "I wonder if I should go help Derek feed and bed down the horses," she mused aloud.

"Do you usually help him?"

"If I'm not helping Mrs. Avery set up the dining room."

"Well, why don't you go help Derek and I'll help Mrs.

Avery," Amy suggested, thinking that any action was preferable to sitting in her room thinking about what she could or would be doing if she were in San Francisco.

Amy hadn't forgotten that she had agreed to have dinner with Frank Jackson, and although that evening he proved to be attentive and an accomplished flirt, he couldn't make up for what she was sure she was missing.

In spite of Frank's good looks and charm, the only real satisfaction she got out of the entire evening was seeing the glowering expression on Derek's face when he came into the dining room to speak to Dick and saw her sitting alone with Frank.

After dinner, Frank suggested they go for a walk, but Amy declined as gently as possible. All night she had made a conscious effort to push aside all thoughts of home and Stephen, but now she just wanted to be alone so she could give in to the desire to think about them.

Unlike the previous night, sleep didn't come quickly, and Amy lay awake for what seemed like hours until she heard Lisa whisper, "Are you awake?"

She considered not answering, but her curiosity got the better of her and she yielded. "Yes."

"Are you hungry?"

Amy pushed herself up on her elbows and stared through the darkness at Lisa. "I could probably eat something. Why? Have you got something to share?"

"No, but I know where we could get something," Lisa said, swinging her legs to the floor. "Let's go raid the kitchen."

Amy hesitated. "Will we get into trouble?"

"Uh-uh. Besides, there are so many people around, no one could possibly notice what we ate."

"That's true," Amy conceded, as she hurried to find her robe and slippers and follow Lisa.

As quietly as possible they made their way through the

house without turning on any lights. Once they were in the kitchen, Lisa closed the door and flipped on the light switch, flooding the kitchen with light so that both girls had to shield their eyes from the brightness.

"What do you feel like?" Lisa asked, standing in front of the refrigerator. "Sweet or salty?"

"Salty, and make it something substantial."

Lisa began pulling out plates. "Here's some fried chicken and roast beef, and I want a piece of this carrot cake."

Amy realized that this was the first time she had felt comfortable with Lisa; somehow, it seemed natural for them to be sharing a midnight snack in the kitchen.

"What's it like living here with all the people coming and going?" she asked between mouthfuls.

Lisa shrugged. "It's all I've ever known. Most of our guests have been coming here for years, and after awhile you get to know them so it's not like having strangers around all the time. Take the Jacksons for instance—I can remember when Frank was short and skinny."

Thinking of the tall, good-looking boy, Amy smiled. "He's changed."

"Yeah, I noticed you two 'noticing' each other," Lisa said teasingly.

Suddenly it occurred to Amy that Lisa might have been interested in Frank herself. "You didn't mind, did you? I mean, he wasn't . . ."

Lisa interrupted her with a laugh. "No, nothing like that. Frank's nice looking and all, but somehow I can't erase the picture of the way he used to be. You wouldn't believe what a spoiled brat he was. I can still remember him throwing himself on the ground and kicking and screaming when he didn't get his way."

"Is that the way it is with all the teenagers who come here? You've known them for so long that now they're like old friends?"

"Pretty much, except . . ." Lisa looked self-conscious.

"There is one that I would really like to date, but either he's too shy or he's just not interested in me." She shook her head and abruptly changed the subject. "Do you have a boyfriend?"

"I don't know," Amy said truthfully. "I was dating someone special."

"The boy in the pictures?"

"Oh, you noticed them?"

Lisa grinned. "How could I miss them? There's a large picture on the dresser, two smaller ones on your bedside table, and one hanging on the wall. At first I thought they were pictures of some movie star, until I realized that I'd never seen him before."

"His name is Stephen Kemp and he's probably the closest thing to a movie star that's ever attended Bay View High. Almost every girl in school has a crush on him, and I'm afraid even to think what might be happening while I'm away."

"Are you afraid he might start dating someone else?"

"I know he will, if I don't get back soon enough." Remembering Derek's reaction, Amy hesitated bringing the subject up, but she wanted to be honest with Lisa. "What would you think if I told you I might go back to San Francisco in the fall?"

Her announcement came as no surprise to Lisa. "Dad told me he gave you a choice."

"Would you mind?"

"I don't know. We're just getting to know each other and I think I'd like you to stay here and live with us, but I understand how you feel. I guess, no matter how many times you move, your real home is wherever you feel you belong."

Amy thought of Lisa's words often during the next few days. She was sure the Sprawling T would never feel like her own home, but she went through the motions without complaint or finding fault, determined that Dick would find nothing in her behavior or attitude to suggest that she wasn't giving the ranch a fair chance. She found that each day was easier than the one before.

Although no one was officially assigned to any particular job, a satisfactory division of labor evolved. Dick was naturally in charge of everything and the final authority on any problem, but beneath him, Maggie supervised the upkeep of the cabins and the kitchen, Derek took care of the horses and the grounds around the lodge, and Amy took on more of the responsibilities of the front desk. Lisa, the most versatile member of the family, helped out in all areas.

Amy soon learned that the front desk was the pulse of the entire ranch. At some time every day, everyone stopped by to pick up or leave messages or just to talk for awhile. Amy's most frequent visitor was Frank Jackson.

She had had dinner with him several times and had even gone swimming with him one afternoon when her schedule permitted it. But between thinking about Stephen, writing letters and postcards to all her friends back home, and trying to learn the routine of the ranch, she hadn't given any thought to developing a relationship with him. Still, she enjoyed the time they spent together.

"I see they have you penned up behind the desk as usual," Frank said, coming in unexpectedly one afternoon.

"Well, hello." She smiled in greeting. "I thought you were on a trail ride."

Frank leaned over the desk until his face was only inches away from hers. "I was, but there wasn't anyone in the group as interesting as someone back here," he said, focusing his dark eyes directly on Amy and pausing pointedly before continuing. "Besides, that guide kept picking on me."

Amy put down the mail she had been sorting through, hoping to find a letter from Stephen, and gave Frank her full attention. "What do you mean?"

"Oh, that boy who takes care of the animals kept claiming that I was being too rough with my horse," Frank said irritably. "All I was doing was trying to get some life out of the old nag. If he'd given me a horse more suitable to my experience in the first place, I wouldn't have had to be so rough."

Even though she hadn't been around long enough to qualify as an authority, Amy felt she owed the ranch her support. "I'm sure he'll give you a different horse the next time if you ask him to."

"He'd better."

The heavy front doors were thrown open with such force that they slammed into the wall, shocking Amy and Frank into silence as Derek entered.

Amy thought she had seen Derek angry before, but that was nothing compared with the way he looked now.

"Frank, I want to talk to you outside, if you don't mind," he said coldly.

Frank turned his back on Derek and without bothering to straighten up said, "I do mind. If you have something to say to me, you can do it right here."

"Fine," Derek said, rapidly closing the space between them and speaking in a deadly calm voice. "I'm giving you notice right now that for the remainder of your visit here this year, you will not be allowed to ride any horse owned by this ranch. Is that clear?"

Frank straightened and faced Derek, but he respected Derek's anger enough to stay clear of him. "No, it isn't. I am a paying guest, and if I'm not mistaken, this ranch is supposed to offer horseback riding."

"Not to anyone who mistreats our animals."

"Awww, I didn't do anything to that old nag that she didn't deserve, and you know it."

"No animal deserves to be treated like that! As far as I'm concerned, the next time you want to go up into the mountains, you can take a hike!"

"We'll just see about that!" Frank's voice rose to a shout as he began moving to the door. "You wait right here and I'll bring my father over to talk to Mr. Thompkins, and we'll see who's right."

Derek's anger was now controlled, and when he spoke again his voice was cool and confident. "You can bring anyone you want to into this, but my order still stands."

Nervously, Amy spoke up. "Dick's upstairs. I'll go get him."

Frank gave her a nod of approval. "At least someone around here knows how to treat a guest."

"Amy can do anything she wants to help you, but it's still not going to change anything," Derek warned.

As Frank went out the front door, Amy hurried upstairs, thankful that she had remembered Dick was in his office. She knocked softly at the door.

"Dick, could you come downstairs for a minute?"

"Do you have a problem?" he asked, putting down his pen and pushing aside the papers he had been working on.

"It's not me. It's Derek."

"Derek?" Dick's brow creased into worry lines. "What happened?"

"He and Frank Jackson got into an argument, and Frank's gone to get his father to talk to you."

Dick got up. "We'd better go find out what this is all about," he said. He followed Amy downstairs where Mr. Jackson and Frank were already waiting.

Derek had been sitting on the sofa, away from the Jacksons, but when Dick came in, he got up and walked over.

Mr. Jackson began. "Dick, I'd like to know why Frank has been told he isn't allowed to ride the horses anymore."

"I don't blame you," Dick said, agreeing affably as he turned to his nephew. "Derek, what can you tell us about this?"

Derek looked at Frank and then back at Dick. "He was

being too rough with his horse, and after I corrected him repeatedly, he left the group and rode back to the lodge alone. When he did that, he took full responsibility for his horse—and that doesn't mean leaving her hot and tired and tied to a fence without food and water.''

"He never said a word to me about mistreating my horse!" Frank denied loudly. "He's just mad because I got back to the lodge before he did . . . and he saw me talking to Amy. He's probably jealous or something."

"That's not true," Derek said quietly.

"It is too! Ask Amy. She can tell you he started yelling at me the minute he walked in.''

Dick looked at his stepdaughter. "Can you tell us anything about what happened?"

Color flooded Amy's face. She hadn't known she was going to be drawn into this, but she could feel all their eyes on her and she had to say something.

"Derek *was* angry when he came in, but . . ."

"See!" Frank snarled.

"Wait." Dick silenced him. "I want her to finish. Go on, Amy.''

"Before Derek came in, Frank told me that Derek had been on him about being too rough with his horse," she finished slowly.

"She's lying to protect him. I just said he was picking on me!" Frank shouted.

"Watch your mouth," Derek warned Frank sharply and then turned to speak directly to Mr. Jackson. "I've told Frank that he isn't allowed to ride anymore and I've explained the reasons. If you'd like to check out his horse yourself, I've got her in a stable in the barn. Now, if you'll excuse me, I'll go take care of the other horses.''

When he had finished, Derek turned on his heel and walked away, leaving the Jacksons staring after him.

"Henry, I'm sorry that something like this has happened," Dick said, "but Derek has been working with our animals for five years, and for the last two he's been totally in charge. When it comes to the horses, he has the final word.''

''I understand,'' Mr. Jackson said and turned to his son. ''Come on, Frank.''

Frank pulled back. ''But Dad! Are you just going to take this? You mean I can't ride?''

''You've just heard two people accuse you of mistreating an animal. Now, come on!''

This time Mr. Jackson meant it; with one last angry glance at Amy, Frank stormed out of the room behind his father.

5

The silence that followed the Jacksons' departure seemed deafening.

"Oh, Dick," Amy said softly, "I'm so sorry."

Dick sighed. "There's no reason for you to apologize, Amy. You didn't do anything."

"But I feel I could have done something to . . ."

Dick interrupted, shaking his head. "If it makes you feel any better, I would have backed Derek even without your support. The only difference you made was to make it easier for Frank's father to accept the truth."

In spite of his assurance, Amy's face still looked pinched and drawn, and Dick suggested, "Why don't you take a break? I'll watch the desk."

Amy let out her breath in one long sigh. "Thanks. I think I'd like to get some fresh air."

Without realizing what she was doing, Amy found herself heading toward the corral.

She found Derek in a stall, applying some salve to the open cuts around the horse's mouth.

"Will she be all right?" Amy asked, coming up behind him.

Derek glanced up at Amy before returning to his task. "She'll live, but she can't be ridden for the next few days or maybe a week. Her mouth is all cut up from the way that jerk was using the bit on her. I suppose you came out here so I could thank you personally for backing me up in there?" he asked spitefully.

As always, Derek's temper had a way of igniting Amy's. "For the record, I wasn't backing you up. I was just telling what I knew."

"Well, whatever it was, it wasn't necessary. I could have handled it myself."

"I know. Dick told me he would have backed you up anyway, but they asked me, so . . ."

"So you made Frank angry with you for nothing."

"After knowing how he lied, do you think I care?"

There was no way she could make Derek understand or believe her reasons, and since she didn't know why she had bothered to try in the first place, Amy turned to leave. As she did, she heard a pitiful noise, something between a child's cry and a board squeaking.

Derek noticed her sudden pause and asked, "What is it?"

"I heard something."

He listened with her for a moment. "Oh, that's just some kittens. Some cats stay around the barn and keep mice and other rodents away, and one of them has probably had a litter."

Now Amy could tell where the sounds were coming from, and she knelt on a bale of hay that was stacked behind the seldom-closed barn door.

"Look," she called to Derek, their recent argument forgotten as she peered down at the squirming balls of fur.

Baby animals were no novelty to Derek, but at her urging he went to take a look. There were four kittens, all with their eyes still tightly shut, moving around blindly in the small bed in the hay, each one trying to mew louder than its sibling.

"What's wrong with them?" Amy asked.

"Nothing. All kittens are born with their eyes closed. They won't open for a week or so."

"Where's their mother?"

"She's around somewhere. She probably went out to find some food for herself."

"You mean she just left them alone? What if something happened to them?"

The corners of Derek's mouth deepened with amusement. "What do you expect her to do? Get a sitter? She'll be back soon. She wouldn't leave them for very long, unless . . ."

His voice held a note of doubt that Amy picked up immediately. "Unless what?" she asked, forcing him to finish his thought.

"This morning James told me that he'd found a dead cat that had lost a fight with a raccoon. He said it looked as if she'd recently had a litter. I hope these aren't hers."

"What are we going to do?"

He shook his head sadly. "First we'll have to wait and see if their own mother returns."

Amy stared at him aghast. "But if James told you about it this morning and it was their mother that got killed, they've already been without food too long! If we wait any longer, they'll die."

"And if it wasn't their mother, we'll have worried for nothing."

He took her arm and pulled her away from the kittens. "Listen, Amy, there must be at least a half a dozen female cats around the barn, and if we took care of each litter they had, there'd be so many cats around here we couldn't walk for stepping on them. They're wild; they can take care of themselves."

From the way Derek was talking, Amy suspected he

didn't intend to do anything. Quickly she evaded his restraining hand and went back to kneel beside the kittens. Without another word she pulled up the bottom of her shirt and, reaching out, she picked up one of the kittens and tenderly placed it in her shirt. It was so tiny its little bones felt like toothpicks, and she could feel its heart beating rapidly beneath the thin layer of flesh.

"What do you think you're doing?" Derek demanded.

Amy reached for another kitten. "Since you obviously don't intend to do anything about them, I'm going to."

"Don't be ridiculous! They're only a few days old. They'll need someone to take care of them twenty-four hours a day, and you don't know the first thing about taking care of newborn kittens. They'll probably die without their mother, anyway."

How could he go to pieces over some cuts on a horse's mouth but condemn four defenseless kittens to death? she thought as she picked up the last two kittens and stood up to face him. "I'm going to take care of them and they aren't going to die!"

Derek put his hand on her arm, but she jerked away. "Don't you dare try to stop me!"

Derek had already decided that if the kittens' mother hadn't returned by the time he left the barn, he would take them home and let Jason take care of them. Jason had more experience in taking care of sick animals and he would be able to accept it if the kittens didn't live, but Derek knew that Amy wasn't about to hand the kittens over to him at this point so he didn't even suggest it.

"I was just going to tell you to call my brother Jason. He knows more about taking care of animals than anyone else I know."

"Thanks," she said stiffly as she headed out of the barn and back to the lodge.

For a minute she stood frozen in the doorway. Dick was still at the desk, and it suddenly occurred to her that he might agree with Derek and refuse to let her bring the kittens inside or insist that she abandon them. Apprehensively, she attempted to explain the entire situation to Dick in just one breath.

"I found some baby kittens whose mother might be dead and Derek was going to wait and see but they're hungry and they might die. Can I keep them and take care of them?"

Amy went over and held out her shirt so that Dick could see the kittens. "Derek said they were only a few days old."

"You know, it's not going to be easy to take care of them," Dick warned, "and they still may not live."

Amy bit her lip. "Derek said that I should call Jason— that he could tell me what to do."

Dick nodded in agreement. "Go find a box to put them in, and I'll call Jason for you."

"Oh, thank you. There are still some boxes from when Mom and I unpacked. I'll go get one of them," she said, hurrying away.

Amy was grateful that Jason cared enough not only to tell her what she should do but to come over and check out the kittens for her.

The first priority was to get some food into them. Over the telephone, he explained how she was to soak a clean washcloth in some warm milk and let the kittens suck at it until he could get there.

It wasn't difficult to get the kittens to cooperate. They were so hungry that the instant they got a taste of the milk, they attacked the washcloth with such vigor Amy was afraid they were going to swallow a piece of the cloth and choke themselves.

No one had mentioned Jason's age, and Amy was disappointed when she discovered how young he was, but as he handled the kittens with infinite care and experience, she found herself trusting him implicitly.

"This cloth won't satisfy them for long. Make a mixture of milk, an egg, and some honey, if you've got it, and pour it into this,'' he said, pulling a miniature bottle from his back pocket.

"Where did you get that?'' she asked. "It looks just like the bottles I had when I played with dolls.''

Jason grinned. "That's just what it is. My sister, Stacy, used to complain that she could never find any of her dolls' bottles. I had stolen them all.''

Amy hurried to mix up the formula just as Jason had instructed. As soon as she had filled the bottle, she rushed back to the hungry kittens, but Jason stopped her before she could pick one up.

Carefully, he marked the bottle off in fourths. "This milk isn't exactly like their mother's, so you'll have to give their systems time to get used to it. Besides, they're so hungry now, they could over-eat and kill themselves. Just give each of them a fourth of the bottle. When they start improving, you can increase it.''

"But will that be enough?'' Amy asked.

"Yeah, if you repeat it every other hour.''

Amy gingerly lifted one of the little kittens. Its pathetic cries wrenched her heart as it searched wildly for the milk. When it discovered the bottle, it latched on to it with more strength than Amy would have thought possible.

She repeated the process with the other three kittens, and only when Jason was ready to leave did she ask, "Do you think they'll live?''

He didn't answer immediately. "They're weak, but I think you got to them in time. What you have to remember is that these cats are bred to be tough. If they make it through the next twenty-four hours and don't develop any complications from the formula, they should do all right; but if you have any problems, night or day, call me.''

"I will, and thank you so much for coming over and bringing the bottle,'' Amy said gratefully.

Before nightfall, everyone in the family and all of the guests had seen the kittens and passed some verdict on them. Amy, totally absorbed by her charges, rushed around showing them off and listening to the advice and comments like any proud mother.

Lisa gave the kittens a cursory glance and asked, "Do you mind if I ask where you plan to keep them?"

"In this box. Jason said it would be fine for now."

"That isn't what I meant. Which *room* are you going to keep them in?"

"Ours. That way, I'll be sure to hear them . . . Don't tell me you're allergic to cats?"

"No, just to the noise they make," Lisa said with a grimace. At the expression on Amy's face, she relented. "Oh, go ahead. It won't kill me to lose a couple of nights' sleep."

As it turned out, that was only her first concession. When Amy started to crawl out of bed for the kittens' three-o'clock feeding, Lisa waved her back.

"This one's on me," she said groggily.

Amy didn't argue. It seemed as though she had just finished their one-o'clock feeding, and she knew with certainty that they would be crying again by five.

When the kittens were still thriving the next morning, everyone began to breathe more easily, confident that they would survive. The news of and concern for the kittens had served to overshadow the incident with Frank Jackson.

Every time the door opened, she dreaded having to face Frank, but although Mr. and Mrs. Jackson and Laura continued with their usual activities, Frank refused to leave the cabin. After two days of his self-imposed confinement, the Jacksons cancelled the rest of their vacation.

The entire episode made Amy think seriously about boys in general. In San Francisco, Stephen had told her that he really cared for her, but it had been almost two weeks since she had written to him and he still hadn't written or called. And Frank Jackson had certainly been a disappointment. Watching him change from a charming friend to a sullen, spoiled jerk had been an eye-opening experience for her. Ironically, it seemed the only boy she could trust not to change was Derek. He continued to be the same arrogant, argumentative person he had been when they'd first met.

For the time being, it seemed easier for her to forget all about boys and concentrate on her kittens. They had continued to grow stronger every day and now that they had finally opened their eyes, Amy spent much of her free time playing with them.

She could already see subtle differences in their personalities and had given them names to match. Grumpy was a little spitfire who instinctively fought against any human contact until the bottle was in his mouth. Bashful was extremely shy and Happy was placid and lovable. The smallest one, she named Dopey because he had trouble keeping the bottle in his mouth and always managed to gag himself when he tried to drink.

However, Amy's preoccupation with the kittens couldn't insulate her from what seemed to be the main interest of everyone else at the ranch. For some reason, she thought, they all took her inability to ride as a personal failure, as if it was somehow their fault. The actual truth of the matter was that she had no burning desire to learn.

She still gave the horses in the corral a wide berth whenever she passed them. They looked so powerful and much too independent. She could never imagine herself riding one, but her mother, Lisa, James, Derek, and even Mr. and Mrs. Avery refused to let the subject rest. Only Dick seemed to understand.

"Amy, I'm very pleased with the way you have accepted the ranch and helped out," he said, "and if you don't want to ride, no one is going to force you."

Knowing she had Dick's support, Amy successfully managed to decline all the offers to teach her to ride until Ricky returned. Ricky's most effective weapon was his charm, and almost before she knew what she was doing,

Amy found herself in a pair of borrowed boots, walking nervously toward the corral and her first riding lesson.

Ricky, a broad smile on his handsome face, was waiting for her. As soon as he saw her, he called to his cousin, "Derek, which horse do you think I should choose for Amy?"

Without pausing to consider the question, Derek answered, "Lady."

"Lady? She's too old! I'll bet even Dick learned to ride on her," Ricky said, not bothering to conceal the disgust in his voice.

Derek shrugged. "You asked my opinion."

For a minute, Ricky looked over the other horses in the corral. "Well, I guess he knows them better than anyone else," he said under his breath, and then raised his voice again. "How about saddling her up while I get my horse?"

Amy watched anxiously as Derek picked a large horse from among several in the corral and brought her to the fence. She looked placid enough, but her shoulder was a foot above Amy's head.

"Don't they come in a smaller size?" she asked.

"Yes, but some of those might want to run or disagree with the way you want to go. Lady's fat because she won't go any faster than a walk, and absolutely nothing you do will upset her," Derek said.

To prove his point, Derek walked completely around the horse, patting and rubbing against her. Lady never even turned her head to look at him.

Ricky had saddled and mounted his horse while Derek took his time and explained everything to Amy.

"Go around to her left side to mount," Ricky told her.

"Why the left side?"

"That's the way it's done," Ricky said.

"With Lady, it wouldn't matter," Derek said, ignoring Ricky's obvious impatience to be on their way. "But it is better for you to learn the correct way from the beginning.

As a general rule, most horses are trained for mounting on the left, and that's what they get used to. Besides, you're going to put your left foot in the stirrup and push off with your right.''

Amy looked at the stirrup hanging from Lady's saddle. "How am I supposed to reach that?"

"Eventually you'll need to learn how to mount from the ground, but today you can use the block," he said, leading Lady to a low platform from which Amy could easily step into the stirrup and swing herself onto the horse's broad back.

"What do I do now?" she asked as she perched high in the saddle.

"Just tap her with your heels to make her go and pull back on the reins when you want to stop," Ricky said.

Automatically, Amy turned to Derek for confirmation and a more complete explanation.

Reassuringly, Derek gave her the instructions she wanted and ended by saying, "Riding a well-trained horse is like taking a walk with a little kid. Pretend the reins are the child's hands and just kind of nudge them along in the direction you want to go. With Lady, you won't even have to worry about that. She'll follow the horse in front of her. She'll stop when he stops and go just fast enough to keep him in sight.''

Just as Ricky turned his horse to head up the trail, Lisa came running out of the lodge. "Ricky, wait!"

Ricky looked over his shoulder, impatient with another delay.

"You have a telephone call. I think it's Ellen," Lisa called breathlessly.

Ricky looked uncertainly from Lisa to Amy. He seemed on the verge of telling Lisa to take a message when Derek said, "Go ahead and take the call. I'll ride with Amy."

The relief of having the situation taken out of his hands was plainly written on Ricky's face, and for once, Amy didn't really care. In contrast to his usual high-handed ways now Derek seemed patient and understanding.

The cousins quickly exchanged places and with just a word to Lady, Derek pointed his horse toward the trail. Lady, amiable as always, followed.

Amy was concentrating so hard on keeping the reins straight but not taut, gripping the saddle with her knees, and keeping her weight properly distributed that she hadn't even noticed how far they had gone when Derek asked, "Do you want to get down and stretch your legs?"

"Yes, I think so."

She waited until Derek dismounted and came around to her. She handed him the reins and, trying to look like an experienced rider, swung her leg over the saddle and jumped softly to the ground, and then ruined the entire effect by having her legs buckle under her.

Derek was standing by ready to catch her. His strong arms steadied her until she regained her balance. "It takes some time for your legs to get use to riding," he said kindly.

"Tell me about it." Amy groaned, attempting a few deep-knee bends to work out the kinks.

"Let's walk awhile," he suggested. "That'll help some."

Amy glanced curiously at Derek out of the corner of her eye. This gentle, considerate side of him was new to her. She would never have thought she could enjoy being alone with him. She tried to take her mind off him by focusing on their surroundings. They had walked out into an open meadow that stretched unbroken to the mountains—there were no fences or boundaries of any kind.

"Is all of this part of the ranch?" she asked.

Derek nodded. "This and more."

"I never realized it was so large."

He grinned. "That's why it's called a ranch. If it were any smaller, it would be a backyard."

"Why doesn't Dick do something with it?" she asked.

"Like what?"

"Develop it."

"You mean sell it for housing projects or shopping malls?" Derek's tone was scornful.

"No, that wasn't what I meant. But why doesn't he put in a golf course and some tennis courts, and maybe even some chair lifts for skiing in the winter? With this much land so close to a tourist area like Lake Tahoe, he could make the ranch a big attraction."

"Why would he want to do that?"

"I would think that's obvious. It would be more profitable."

They had stopped walking to face each other.

"Profit isn't everything. There's something to be said for keeping the land unspoiled. Dick has everything he needs, so why should he rip up all this just to make a few more dollars?" Derek asked.

"If he planned it right, he wouldn't have to 'rip up' or 'spoil' anything. And it's not just the money. It's . . . being the best. That's the American way, isn't it? If you're going to plant a garden, build a house, or run a guest ranch, it just seems that you'd want it to be the very best you could possibly make it. Why settle for less?"

"Amy, look around you. How can you call all this natural beauty settling for less?"

They had been standing in one spot for too long; Derek's horse stamped his feet impatiently. Derek broke off what he was going to say with a shake of his head. It was obvious that he wasn't going to change her mind about the ranch. "Are you ready to go back?"

"Yes," she said shortly.

He nodded toward Lady. "Do you want me to help you get back in the saddle?"

"No, I'll do it myself."

It proved to be even more difficult than she had expected.

But Lady held perfectly still while Amy made a few awkward attempts to get her foot in the stirrup and boost herself off the ground. Finally, in desperation, she grabbed the saddle horn and practically crawled up the horse's side.

When her feet were securely in the stirrups again, she nodded to Derek. "I'm ready."

Abruptly, Derek turned his horse around, presenting his back to Amy. Ostensibly it was so that he could lead the way back to the lodge, but once his face was hidden, he let the grin, which had been lurking at the corners of his mouth, spread across his face. He still thought she was wrong about making changes to the ranch, but she had looked so darn proud of herself for mounting Lady, something his five-year-old brother could have done with ease, that he had to smile.

Behind him, Amy was digging holes in his back with her eyes. She hadn't meant her suggestions to make him angry. After all, almost everything could stand some improvement. Why did he have to take everything so personally!

They rode back to the lodge in silence, and Amy was relieved to see Dick and Ricky waiting at the corral. At least with them around, she wouldn't have to speak to Derek.

"I'm sorry I didn't get to go with you," Ricky said apologetically, coming over to help her down.

"That's all right. I think it went okay," she said, smiling.

"I'll say it did," Dick said approvingly.

Ricky took the reins from her. "I'll take care of Lady for you. We'll let you have a few more lessons before you have to start taking care of your own horse."

"Thanks. I think what I'd like now is something soft to sit on."

Without a word or backward glance at Derek, Amy returned to the lodge, where she found her mother and Mrs. Avery poring over some lists.

"How was your first lesson?" her mother asked.

"Fine, I think, but I want to soak in a hot tub," Amy answered.

"Go ahead, but don't take too long. I want you to watch the desk while I go into Truckee with Mrs. Avery. We need to restock the kitchen," Maggie said and then added, "By the way, you got a letter from Shannon."

Amy paused on the stairs. "Is that all?"

Her mother had already turned her attention back to the grocery lists, but at Amy's question, she looked up again. "Yes. Were you expecting something else?"

"No," Amy said. "I guess not. Just put Shannon's letter on the desk. I'll read it when I come down."

6

Amy waited until her mother and Mrs. Avery had left before she opened the letter from Shannon. Later she would read it carefully, going over every line, but now she scanned the pages, looking for any mention of Stephen. Finally she found what she was looking for:

Stephen was at Jeannette's party last week. He didn't bring a date, but he seemed to have fun dancing with every girl there. I told him that I had talked to you and that you seemed happy at the ranch, but today when we played tennis, he told me that you had written him that you were coming back to San Francisco. Is that true? Let me know as soon as possible!

Amy reread the paragraph. ". . . we played tennis . . ." Did that mean Shannon and Stephen had met at the courts accidentally or had they arranged it? A date? Shannon and Stephen!

Even if Stephen didn't know how strongly she felt about him, Shannon certainly did, and the betrayal, if that's what it was, cut deeply.

Amy stared at the switchboard. It seemed to be fate that she was at the desk, alone, with the means of calling Shannon so conveniently close at hand. She knew she shouldn't make any long-distance calls without permission, but she did have her allowance and there certainly hadn't been anything else to spend it on. Besides, this was an emergency. She would die if she didn't find out what was going on.

She dialed Shannon's number and got her friend on the third ring.

"I just got your letter," Amy said.

"Amy!" Shannon cried, "Is it true? Are you coming back?"

Amy pretended innocence. "Didn't I tell you? Dick said I might be able to when the summer's over."

"That's . . . great."

Amy wondered if the hesitation she thought she heard in Shannon's voice was only in her own head. She wanted desperately to ask about Stephen but forced herself to wait. If she wanted the truth, it would have to come voluntarily from Shannon.

"I thought I'd written you about it in my last letter, but I've been so busy, I don't know whether I'm coming or going. Would you believe that I'm learning to ride a horse and that I've adopted four motherless kittens?"

Her nervousness was making her voice unnaturally high, and she knew she was talking too fast, but Shannon didn't seem to notice.

"I'm really glad you called, but I know we can't talk very long and I have something important to ask you," Shannon said and took a deep breath before she continued. "Stephen said he asked you to go steady and that you turned him down. Does that mean . . ."

Amy gripped the receiver tighter. "What?"

"I guess I'm trying to say that the rules we made for each other concerning boyfriends are getting a little blurred. If you wouldn't go steady with Stephen, does that mean he's up for grabs? You know I wouldn't do anything behind your back."

"If you want Stephen, you're welcome to him," Amy said curtly, her words sounding clipped and hurt to her own ears.

Shannon chose to ignore the unspoken plea. "Do you mean it?"

"Of course I do." Amy forced a laugh that was too high and artificial. "Since my first week here, I haven't even had time to think about Stephen."

"Oh?" Shannon's voice contained the slightest hint of doubt.

Desperately, Amy conjured up a picture of Ricky. "Actually, I've been seeing this fantastic boy who works at the ranch. He's the one who's teaching me to ride."

"I should have known that you'd never sit at home," Shannon said.

The front doors opened and Amy looked up to see Lisa. "Someone just came in, so I'll have to go. I'll write you later," she said quickly into the telephone before hanging up.

"You didn't have to hang up on my account," Lisa protested.

"I didn't," Amy said distractedly. "Not really, anyway. The call was a mistake in the first place, and I was looking for an excuse to end it."

"Oh," Lisa said understandingly and dropped the subject. "Were you here when the Johnsons checked in?"

Amy shook her head. "No, but I've only been here a few minutes. Why?"

Lisa pulled the registration book over and pointed to the name. "They must have checked in earlier," she said and explained. "Their son asked me about going to pan for gold. I might as well take him tomorrow, since I don't have anything else planned."

"You can find gold around here?"

Lisa grinned. "It's nothing to start another gold rush over, but there's some color in the streams above Star Lake. It gets washed down when the snow melts every year. Do you want to come with us?"

"Would I have to ride . . ."

"A horse?" Lisa finished for her. "Yes, but you could take Lady again. C'mon and go with us. You might like it."

Anything was better than sitting around worrying about Shannon and Stephen, Amy thought. And the worst possible thing for her to do right now was to take any action—not until she had thought through the whole situation and decided on a plan. Besides, maybe she'd find a nugget. That would certainly be something to take back to San Francisco with her.

The next morning, while Amy finished feeding her kittens and reminded her mother—three times—to check on them while she was gone, Lisa and Mark Johnson saddled the horses and got the equipment ready.

"You follow Lisa, and I'll ride behind you in case you have any problems," Mark said.

His suggestion was practical, but not one that suited Lady. Twice Mark pulled up his horse to let Lady pass him, but both times Lady stopped and waited for Mark to continue before falling in behind him again.

They were taking the steeper, more treacherous trail that led past Star Lake to one of the streams formed by the runoff of the winter's snow. The ride should have taken less than an hour, but with the slower pace that Lady preferred it was well over an hour before Lisa signaled them to stop.

Amy was eager to dismount. It was the longest ride she had taken, and though Lady had never faltered, there were times when Amy gripped the saddle horn with both hands and clenched her eyes shut.

"What do we do now?" she asked, walking around gingerly to get the feel of firm ground beneath her once again.

"We look for gold," Lisa answered jokingly.

Mark splashed ahead of them into the stream and let out a whoop as the icy water soaked through his pants legs. "You'd better walk in slowly," he warned Amy. "It takes a while to get used to it."

He made his way back to the edge of the stream and waited until Amy joined him. When she slipped on the first smooth stone, he was there to steady her and kept his hand under her arm until she became accustomed to the cold water and could move about without trembling.

For a minute Amy stood watching the water rushing madly around her legs. It was so clear she could see straight to the bottom of the stream. Without realizing what she was doing, she began scanning the bottom for gold nuggets.

Lisa glanced back at her and laughed out loud. "It's not quite that easy!"

Mark hurried over with an extra pan. "Here, I'll show you how to do it," he said.

He bent over and scooped up a pan full of water, sand, and gravel. Gently, almost tenderly, he began to swirl the pan, letting the sand slide over the side and studying the bottom of the pan for any sign of color. It was hard to say which one of them was more excited when his third panning revealed some tiny flecks.

"Gold!" they shouted simultaneously.

Now that she had some idea of what she was supposed to do, Amy began panning for gold with determination, but even that couldn't match the experience of Lisa or Mark, and though none of them found a significant amount of the precious metal, Amy's meager haul was the least.

"Here," Mark offered, "you can have mine."

"Oh, I couldn't," Amy protested, rubbing her aching back. "You worked too hard for that. Besides, I can always come back. Maybe next time, I'll be lucky and find a nugget."

Amy kept busy working at the desk, taking care of her kittens, and eventually even going on some of the trail rides with the guests, but at night, when she was alone, she couldn't help thinking about Shannon and Stephen.

After the first wave of anger and jealousy had passed, she tried to examine her feelings calmly and rationally. She was angry at Shannon for going after Stephen, especially as Shannon knew that Amy was returning, and she was hurt that Stephen's feelings for her were so shallow that he hadn't bothered to get in touch with her.

Irrationally she considered writing to both of them that she had no intention of ever coming back to San Francisco and that she never wanted to see either of them again. But that wasn't true. She wanted desperately to go back and pick up exactly where she had left off.

There wasn't anything she could do about Stephen. She had already written him, and until he responded her hands were tied. She couldn't let him know how much she wanted to hear from him because one thing she knew with certainty —the quickest way to bore Stephen was to be too available. But she *had* to find out what was happening between him and Shannon so that she would know how to deal with it once she returned.

Obviously then, the only thing left for her to do was to make Shannon think that she really didn't care about Stephen any longer. Fortuitously, she had already planted the seeds for her idea in her last conversation with Shannon. She had mentioned seeing another boy, so all she had to do was let Shannon know that she was serious about someone else and before she knew it, Shannon would be revealing everything about her relationship (or lack of it) with Stephen.

Now that she had decided on a plan, Amy got out her stationery. She wanted her letter to sound natural and casual, so she wrote quickly, without too much deliberation:

Dear Shannon,

I'm sorry I cut you off so quickly on the phone the other day, but I didn't think it was a very good idea to be caught discussing an old boyfriend in front of a new one—if you know what I mean. I have met someone *very* special, and I don't want anything to go wrong.

I don't blame you at all for dating Stephen. He is the cutest thing in the Bay area, and now that he's available, why should you let some other girl snap him up?

I'll keep you posted on all the latest developments here, and you do the same. I hope everything works out for both of us.

Love,
Amy

Satisfied that the letter seemed direct and sincere, Amy put it in the mail and prepared herself to wait for more news so that she could adjust her plans accordingly.

While she waited, she allowed herself to be drawn into a pattern of uncomplicated days that were varied enough to be interesting, but with enough constancy so that she was able to feel comfortable with the routine.

The average guest, she learned, stayed about a week. Most of them were either middle-aged couples who wanted to get away from the city and do a little fishing or just play cards and relax with other guests, or they were young couples with noisy children who kept the staff busy with riding lessons, trail rides, panning for gold, fishing, hiking, and swimming. The smallest percentage of their guests were teenagers.

By the time Mark Johnson and his family left, the

Robertsons and their two teenage daughters arrived, and later that same week, the Stokeses, including sixteen-year-old Charlie, came.

Ricky continued to be a bright spot in her life. He would stop by the desk to see her almost every day. Sometimes he'd take a minute to play with the kittens or just chat with her about his latest escapades.

The Robertson girls, Eve and Renee, spent their days following Derek and Ricky—when he was there—around the corral or sunning themselves beside the pool, but Charlie, who even charitably couldn't be called anything but plain, was good-natured and pleasant to have around. He had a good sense of humor and won Amy's undying gratitude by helping her construct a safe, comfortable pen for her kittens.

They had outgrown their box, and Amy didn't like leaving them in such a confined area, but she was too concerned for their safety to let them run around freely outside. Besides, they still needed to be fed at least four times a day, and she didn't always have time to search for them.

Derek donated the lumber and wire from his father's hardware store, and Charlie scrounged around until he came up with the necessary tools to build them a large cage that was placed outside the kitchen door where the kittens could enjoy the sunshine. He even designed a pull-out litter box in one corner of the cage so that the kittens would have, as he explained it, indoor plumbing.

Although she had fought against learning to ride, Amy had to admit that she had begun to look forward to going out on trail rides. Only occasionally did she resent always having to bring up the rear, but Lady wouldn't be urged out of her spot, not even when it meant that Derek could single her out for attention.

Usually, Amy limited her rides to the small groups that Lisa led, but one day Derek took Lisa's place at the last minute and Amy had no choice but to stay with the group.

The ride had gone smoothly, so Amy was relaxed when Derek let the other riders pass by him and fell into line beside her.

"Are you doing all right?" he asked.

Amy glanced at him warily. Any conversation with Derek was likely to end in an argument, but since he had been unusually pleasant that day, she let her guard down and smiled. "With Lady, it's impossible to get into any trouble."

He grinned, almost to himself. "Maybe we should figure out some way to tie you to her saddle and keep you there," he said dryly.

Immediately, Amy's guard went back up. "What do you mean by that?"

"Maybe I shouldn't bring it up, but the Hardys are coming to the ranch next month. Since Ray Hardy and Lisa are both kind of shy, it's hard to tell, but I think they like each other, and I guess what I'm really asking is that you leave him alone."

Amy stared at him in disbelief. "Leave him alone! You make me sound like some kind of barracuda!"

"You have to admit, you've managed to attract the attention of every boy who's been around here this summer," he pointed out.

Amy took a deep breath and let it out in a rush. "Not every boy—after all, I certainly haven't attracted you, and who knows, maybe Ray Hardy will feel the same way about me that you do. Then he won't have any trouble staying out of my clutches."

A look of surprise lit Derek's eyes before he masked it with anger and kicked his horse into a trot that left Amy behind.

This time, Derek's anger was directed at himself. He should have known better than to try to explain to Amy about Lisa and Ray, but he had watched the way all the boys had flocked around Amy all summer, and he didn't think that Lisa would have a chance with Ray.

What if Ray did feel the same way about Amy as he did? He didn't even know what his feelings were. Somehow, every time he got near her, she managed to irritate or anger him, but he couldn't seem to stay away.

7

Amy's immediate reaction, once she had recovered from Derek's snide remarks, was to find Lisa and demand to know if Ray Hardy was the boy she liked, but there were always too many people around. Amy couldn't seem to find just the right moment to bring the subject up until after everyone had gone to bed and she and Lisa sneaked downstairs for a snack.

Amy waited until they had filled their plates and sat down at the table before she brought up Ray's name. As soon as she did, she knew she had hit on the truth, for Lisa's usual self-assurance was visibly shaken.

"How did you guess?" Lisa asked.

Amy decided against revealing that Derek had been the one who told her. She knew Lisa wouldn't appreciate knowing that other people were aware of her feelings, and although Derek's method had been crude and insensitive, at least he had meant well.

"You did say you liked someone who came here, and I

remembered how happy you were that they had called for a reservation. Is he the one?''

Lisa nodded. ''For all the good it does me. He doesn't see me as anything but a friend.''

''Have you tried to change that?''

''I wouldn't know how to begin.''

Lisa brought her shoulders up and let them slump forward unhappily. ''I've watched you with some of the boys this summer. You stand around looking confused and uncertain, and they just fall all over themselves to help you. That works for you because it's natural, but I couldn't get away with that. Ray would think I'd lost my mind.''

Amy smiled at the idea of capable, competent Lisa pretending to be helpless. ''No, whatever you do, you don't want to look phony,'' she agreed. ''Tell me something about Ray.''

Lisa had been reluctant to open a conversation about Ray, but now that Amy had brought up the subject, she was happy to have someone to talk to about him. Ray and his father had been coming to the ranch for four years, and during that time, Lisa had learned everything there was to know about him.

She was still talking when they had finished their snacks and made their way back to their room.

''I wish I could give you some advice, but considering the luck I've had with my own boyfriend, I'm probably the last person you should listen to,'' Amy said.

''What do you mean?''

''Stephen is already dating someone else.''

''Are you sure?''

Amy shook her head. ''Not really, but I'm expecting another letter from Shannon, my best friend in San Francisco. I'll know for sure then.''

Lisa crawled into bed and settled down under the covers. She was so quiet that Amy thought she'd gone to sleep, until her voice came out of the darkness. ''I'm glad Dad never got around to putting up a partition in this room.''

"Me too," Amy said.

The shared confidences of their late-night conversations seemed to signal a new beginning to their relationship. Now Amy and Lisa found they had a lot to talk about and sought each other out all during the day, to laugh or commiserate with each other over something.

So Amy wasn't surprised when Lisa stopped by the desk a few days later and asked, "How about riding to Aunt Helen's with me? I have to make a delivery."

"Sure. Mom's upstairs. Let me check to see if she can watch the desk."

"Okay. I'll go get our horses and meet you at the corral."

When Amy got to the corral, Lisa had already saddled both of their horses and had strapped on full saddlebags behind the saddles.

"What are those for?" Amy asked curiously.

"The packs?" Lisa grinned. "Aunt Helen sent word to me to bring over as much tomato juice as we could spare."

"But you must have at least ten large cans in there," Amy said, studying the bulging packs. "What would she want with all that?"

"She didn't say, but I imagine someone needs to take a bath in it."

"Lisa Thompkins, will you please tell me what on earth you're talking about."

"Get on your horse. I'll tell you on the way over there."

A few minutes later, the girls were on their way, the clanking cans reminding them of their purpose, and Lisa started explaining.

"Somebody at Aunt Helen's must have had a run-in with a skunk. The best thing for cutting the odor is tomato juice. You have to literally take a bath in it. I know it sounds funny, but it does work."

"I've never heard of such a thing."

"That's probably because you don't run into many skunks in San Francisco," Lisa observed.

Amy made a face. "That's what you think. Only the kind we run into is the two-legged variety, and you can't get rid of them with a bath of tomato juice."

They topped a small rise and looked down on a long, low ranch house that was surrounded by a white rail fence and had a small corral beside it.

Lisa and Amy were still some distance away when they heard a shout. "Mama! They're here!"

The tall, slim woman, wearing jeans and a T-shirt who came out to meet them didn't look old enough to have children Derek and Jason's ages, not to mention the four others that Amy had heard about. Even closer, when Amy could see the scattered gray in her hair and the laugh lines around her eyes, Helen Jansen looked surprisingly young.

"Aunt Helen, this is Amy, Maggie's daughter," Lisa said, by way of introduction.

Helen's smile was genuine. "Hello, Amy. I've heard a lot about you from Derek and Jason. I'm glad I finally got to meet you."

"Thank you," Amy said, liking her immediately but thinking that if Mrs. Jansen had listened to Derek, she probably hadn't heard anything good about her.

"Did someone run into a skunk?" Lisa asked.

Helen took two cans of tomato juice from Lisa and began punching holes in them with the can opener she had brought out with her. "Yes, and a pretty potent one at that. I have Derek sitting in the old water trough behind the barn."

"You mean Derek was the one who got it?" Lisa asked.

Helen smiled in spite of her attempt not to, "And he's furious about it. Adam told him there was a rabbit caught in one of Jason's old traps and asked Derek to get him out. Derek didn't find out it was really a skunk until he lifted the lid, and then it was too late."

"Is Adam still alive?" Lisa asked incredulously.

"Yes, but only because he's been staying out of Derek's way," Helen said as she handed the opened cans to Amy.

"Would you mind taking these behind the barn and pouring them over Derek? That is, if you can stand the smell."

"Sure," she said, giving Mrs. Jansen her sweetest smile.

Amy followed her nose as the sickening scent got stronger and stronger, but as she started around the barn, she stopped. "Derek," she called, "are you decent?"

There was a long pause before he answered. "Amy? Oh, great . . . that's all I need." He gave a long, audible sigh. "You don't have to worry about being shocked. I still have my clothes on."

He had obviously made a futile attempt to wash the odor away with a strong detergent and water. He stood in the trough soaked to the skin from his head down to his bare feet. "So help me, if you so much as crack a smile, I'm going to grab you and rub this skunk oil all over you."

Amy coughed to cover the laughter that was already bubbling up inside her. "Your mother said I was to pour this over you, so you're going to have to sit down," she managed to say with a straight face.

With a final threatening glare, he sat.

Amy began pouring the juice over his head and watched delightedly as the liquid oozed through his dark hair, making little red riverlets down his face. Derek squinted up at her with one eye closed, and suddenly, without warning, a giggle broke through her control.

Immediately, he grabbed the sides of the trough and started to get up. "Amy, I mean it! I'll have you smelling just like this!"

Believing him, Amy stepped back quickly. "Derek, if you want the rest of this on you, sit down and behave."

Helen and Lisa came around the barn carrying the other cans of juice. "Yes, sit down and let us get the rest of this on you," his mother said.

"So help me, when I catch Adam, I'm going to string him up by his toes!"

Adam, a pint-sized version of his brother, had taken

courage from the presence of Lisa and Amy and had edged up to the trough where Derek was submitting to the shower of juice.

"I'm sorry, Derek. I didn't know what else to do. I couldn't leave him in the trap," he said.

"You could have told me it was a skunk. Then at least I could have used a stick or a rope to pull the trap off him and I wouldn't have been sprayed."

"I guess I didn't think about that," Adam said.

Looking at his brother's worried face, Derek forgave him. "Oh, it's all right. I don't guess I'll smell like this forever. Go get my robe. I'll shuck these clothes and rinse off under the hose before I go inside to take another bath," he said.

Adam hurried off, eager to do whatever he could to get back into Derek's good graces.

"When you finish, just leave those clothes soaking in the tomato juice," Helen said before turning to the girls. "Why don't we go inside and have something to drink?"

The inside of the house was as inviting and comfortable as the outside. Despite the normal clutter that was created by a family of eight, it was clean and smelled pleasantly of home-baked bread.

"Where is everyone?" Lisa asked. "I thought this might be a good time to introduce Amy to the family."

"You'd think that with six children, I should have more of them around, wouldn't you?" Helen laughed. "But the trick seems to be remembering where they all get off to. Let's see, Theresa is in Truckee having lunch with her future mother-in-law, Matt is with John at the store, Jason went fishing, and Stacy is spending the night with a friend. That leaves me with Adam and Derek."

"It sounds as if you need a sign-out sheet to keep track of them," Amy said.

"It's in the hall beside the telephone." Helen grinned. "Why don't you girls stay for dinner? Everyone except Stacy should be back by then."

Amy and Lisa exchanged a quick, inquiring glance, and Lisa said, "I'll go call the ranch and see if it's all right. I'll have to ask Dad and Maggie if they think they can handle everything while their three best hands are all over here."

While Lisa went to make the call, Helen asked, "Are all the cabins rented now?"

"Not this week, but we're booked solid for the next three weeks. We won't have another opening before the middle of August."

"How is the work going?"

Lisa, having gotten their parents' permission to stay, was back in time to hear the last question. "It's been fine," she said. "You can't imagine what a difference Amy and Maggie have made."

"If you get swamped, you know you can count on us to help out. With Theresa's wedding set for Labor Day weekend, she and I will be pretty busy for the rest of the summer, but Matt and Jason can help."

"We'll remember," Lisa assured her.

Jason got home from his fishing trip at the same time that his father and Matt returned from the store. The brothers and their fathers enjoyed a good laugh at Derek's expense, but Amy noticed that they were careful to keep their laughter low so that Derek wouldn't hear.

Theresa was the last to come home, and she arrived in a flurry of activity. She brought in an armful of boxes, swatches of material, and a headful of ideas that she wanted to share with everyone immediately. She paused long enough to be introduced to Amy.

"You must think I'm crazy, and believe me, planning a wedding is enough to make you that way," she said, laughing.

"I think it all sounds wonderful," Amy said, caught up in the romance of the big fairy-tale wedding that Lisa and Helen had described.

"So did I when Dennis proposed, but since then I've

learned that putting a wedding together is a lot of hard work. You wouldn't believe the list of do's and don'ts,'' Theresa said as she collapsed into a chair.

"If you ask me, it's all ridiculous," Derek said.

"No one asked you," Amy said.

"Theresa asked me to be part of the wedding," Derek pointed out.

"But that's different. Unless you object to marriage itself or you really dislike the groom, you should be willing to do anything the bride wants you to because it's important to her.''

"Way to go!" Theresa shouted, giving her an enthusiastic hug. "Amy, I've already selected my wedding attendants, but I would love to have you too. How about it?''

"She'll do anything you want her to do, and you have all the witnesses you need," Derek said with a grin.

Amy couldn't help smiling. "I'd love to be included."

Theresa turned to Lisa. "Why don't you and Amy stay after dinner? The other bridesmaids are coming over and as long as everyone's here, we could go ahead and decide on your dresses.''

"We can't. Amy and I rode over on horseback, so we'll have to get home before dark," Lisa reminded her.

"I wish you could. I don't get to see you that much these days. And I'll see even less of you after I'm married.''

Derek spoke up. "Lisa, why don't you spend the night? That will give you girls a chance to talk. You could bring my jeep back to the ranch tomorrow morning, and I'll ride your horse back with Amy and sleep there in the bunkhouse.''

"You don't have to do that," Amy said. "I know the way back to the lodge, and I can tell Mom and Dick that Lisa's spending the night.''

"You don't ride well enough to go out alone," Derek said.

When Derek used that no-nonsense tone, Amy knew

better than to argue any further, so she gave up the attempt and settled back to enjoy the meal.

Dinner was a relaxed, noisy affair, with everyone laughing and talking at once. Amy forgot all about the time until Derek reminded her.

"We'd better think about getting you and the horses home. It's going to be dark soon."

"Yes, I guess we'd better," she said reluctantly. She was having such a good time she hated to leave, but unfortunately the horses weren't equipped with headlights.

"Tell Dad I'll be home right after breakfast," Lisa said.

"And come back to see us," Helen said. Theresa joined in. "Yes, I may need some more help shaping this group up for the wedding."

As Derek and Amy walked out to the corral where the horses had been unsaddled and left to rest, he asked, "Do you want me to saddle Lady for you?"

"No, thank you. I can saddle her myself," she said proudly.

He gave her a slanted grin. "You think you're pretty good, huh?"

Amy laughed. "No, I think Lady is. I still wouldn't try to saddle just any horse, but Lady's so patient and understanding."

She patted the old horse's flank affectionately. "How did she get such an appropriate name, anyway?"

"I don't know. I guess she's always behaved like a lady, except she's not temperamental."

Amy rose to the bait. "Oh, and in your experience are ladies temperamental?"

"I haven't had a lot of experience, but yes, I guess so," he said.

"Maybe they just seem that way because you're so stubborn."

"Maybe." Derek shrugged as he double-checked to see that Amy had tightened the cinch properly before he allowed her to mount.

The sun was beginning to sink behind the mountains and it gave off varied shades of pink and gold. "Derek, do you ever take guests on overnight camping trips? You know, sleeping under the stars and all that?" Amy asked.

Derek shook his head. "No, not that I can ever recall."

"Why not? I think it would be great. You could take some food and cook over a fire and sleep out in the open. I bet they'd love it."

He grinned in spite of himself. "There you go again. Trying to change things."

"But it is a good idea, isn't it?" she insisted.

"Yeah, I have to admit it is. We'll have to talk to Dick about it and try it out on a few carefully selected guests."

When they came within view of the barn, Lady, anxious for the food she knew would be waiting, picked up more speed than she had shown in the last ten years. Amy laughed aloud at the old horse's enthusiasm.

Her laughter made Derek acutely aware of how quiet and empty the ranch would seem when she left. He dismounted quickly and hurried over to stand beside Lady. When Amy slid off the horse, she was trapped between Lady's side and Derek, who stood only inches away.

Derek cleared his throat but couldn't quite get rid of the lump that gave his voice a strangely husky quality. "Amy, is there any reason to think you might have changed your mind about this place? That you might decide to stay here?"

For a second, Amy was taken aback by the intensity of Derek's gaze, but then a picture of Stephen flashed through her mind. "No, I don't think so," she said softly.

His eyes, which had been warm and strangely vulnerable, suddenly turned remote, as if a door had been slammed shut. "That's what I thought," he said flatly.

Amy was puzzled over the sudden change in his mood. Since she couldn't understand it, she tried to ignore it and turned her attention to Lady. She had reached out to throw the stirrup over Lady's saddle and loosen the cinch when Derek stopped her.

"Go on to the lodge. I'll take care of the horses."

"That's all right. I'll help," she said.

Derek took a deep breath and let it out slowly. "Amy, just go on and tell Dick and Maggie where Lisa is. Here at the Sprawling T, the guests just ride the horses—the hired hands take care of them," he said.

8

Amy's letter to Shannon had accomplished exactly what she thought it would. In her next letter, Shannon was bursting with questions about Amy's new romance and extremely happy to report that she and Stephen were a real "item."

At least this time Amy had prepared herself. She had already accepted her premonitions as fact, and seeing it in print only served to confirm her suspicions.

Lisa saw her reading the letter and stopped to ask, "Did you find out what you wanted to know?"

Amy folded the letter carefully and replaced it in the envelope. "I found out, but it wasn't exactly what I wanted to know."

"Did Shannon know who Stephen was dating?"

Amy nodded. "I guess you could say that. He's dating Shannon."

"Oh, Amy, your best friend! How awful!"

Amy couldn't stand the pity she saw in Lisa's eyes and

tried to cover her own pain with an indifferent shrug. "It's all right. I have a plan. I'll tell you about it after I see how it works."

Amy had been so sure of what she would learn in Shannon's letter that she had already written a rough draft of her reply. Despite numerous interruptions at the desk, she was able to copy it onto her best stationery and get it off in the afternoon mail.

In her letter, Amy described her life on the ranch in glowing terms, but she concentrated mainly on her new boyfriend. To give her story just the right touch of authenticity, Amy pictured herself dating someone like Ricky.

She described the long horseback rides they had taken, having dinner with him and his family, and working alongside him at the ranch so realistically that when Ricky stopped by the desk to see her, she was almost too embarrassed to look him in the eye.

As always when she was troubled, she threw herself into her work to forget her problems, and she didn't have to look very hard to find something to keep her busy. The summer season had reached its peak, and the activity at the ranch had increased considerably.

Now, instead of sitting behind the desk waiting for someone to ask for help, Amy was juggling several phone calls at once, keeping track of which guests had requested extra towels in their cabins, who wanted to go on trail rides or fishing, and how many people would be eating in the dining room that day.

When it became obvious that Lisa and Derek couldn't keep up with all the demands on their time, Derek brought Matt and Jason over to help out. Jason eagerly took over the care of the horses in the corral, and Matt, though less enthusiastic, proved to be a capable guide.

With their days so busy, Lisa and Amy fell exhausted into bed at night, too tired even to consider raiding the kitchen. The only break they had from all the feverish activity was during the dinner hour. While most of the guests were in the dining room, Lisa and Amy took advantage of the almost empty pool to go for a swim.

The days seemed to fly by until, as suddenly as it had started, the rush was over. The normal activity of the ranch seemed slow and lazy by comparison.

"I'll bet it really seems quiet around here when the summer's over and everyone leaves," Amy said to Lisa on the way to the kitchen the first night they resumed their midnight raids.

"It's not too bad. By then, school's ready to start and you know how that is," Lisa said. "With homework, school functions, and the usual chores that have to be done, things never come to a standstill. And, of course, there's always the fall roundup to look forward to."

"What's that?"

"We round up all the cows and separate the ones we're going to sell from the breeding stock, and then we have to dip and vaccinate them and brand the new ones. It takes about a week and it's a lot of hard work, but I love it. I felt so grown up the first time Dad let me help."

"Do you think he'd let me?"

"Sure, if you're still here."

They hadn't talked about Amy leaving, and the possibility that had seemed so distant in June now loomed close at hand. Amy was aware of a sudden sinking sensation, which she attributed to her problem with Shannon.

"I may not be able to go back," she said.

"What do you mean?"

"Shannon has been writing me all about her wonderful romance with Stephen. She was even invited to spend the Fourth-of-July weekend with him and his family in Monterey. It's all very cozy."

Lisa paused, her sandwich halfway to her mouth. "You mean Shannon writes you all about her dates with your boyfriend? Doesn't she know how much she's hurting you?"

"No. That was my plan. I told her that I had a new boyfriend up here."

"Why on earth did you do that?"

"So she'd keep writing me and telling me everything she and Stephen were doing."

"Why would you want to know?"

"So I would know what I had to do to break them up and get Stephen back."

"Do you still want to get him back?"

"Of course!"

Lisa was totally confused and didn't try to hide it. "But if he's dating Shannon, why aren't you angry with him too? Isn't he as much to blame as she is?"

Amy had tried not to think about that. "It's not the same," she said, rationalizing it. "For one thing, I never told Stephen how I felt about him. My strategy was to keep him guessing, never letting him know how much I cared, so that he wouldn't take me for granted."

"After you get back and you manage to take Stephen away from Shannon, what are you going to do then? Are you going to tell him how you feel, or are you going to just keep playing games with him?"

Amy hadn't thought that far ahead. "I don't know," she admitted.

"Is he really worth all the trouble you're going through?"

Amy nodded. "There isn't a girl at Bay View High School who wouldn't give her eyeteeth to have Stephen Kemp as her boyfriend."

"Is that why you want him?"

"That isn't fair!" Amy said, standing up abruptly and taking her plate to the sink. "I just can't explain it. Can you explain why you like Ray?"

"No, I guess not, but at least you'll have a chance to help me figure it out tomorrow."

Amy turned around quickly. "Tomorrow! Really? I can't

believe I forgot all about checking the registration book to see who's coming tomorrow.''

Lisa grinned. "That's probably because you've had your hands full just trying to keep track of the Barnette boys."

"Don't even mention them." Amy groaned.

This was the first year that the Barnettes had visited the ranch, and the consensus of opinion of everyone who had been around their overactive nine-year-old triplets was that there might not be a ranch after they left. So far, they had destroyed three pillows in a pillow fight, broken at least one dish per child at every meal, and stopped up the drain in the swimming pool—and they had been there only one day.

"Come on," Amy said to Lisa. "Between keeping an eye on those little imps and watching for the Hardys' arrival, we're going to have a big day tomorrow. We'd better get to bed."

The Barnette triplets were the first to show up for breakfast the next morning. Lisa whispered to Amy, "Do you think we should send someone to their cabin to make sure their parents aren't gagged and bound to their bed?"

"Are you kidding? Their parents are probably the ones who threw them out," Amy whispered back.

"I can't say that I would blame them," Lisa said, picking up the list of guests who had signed up for a trail ride.

"Do you want to trade places with me so that you'll be here when the Hardys arrive?" Amy asked.

"I'd be very tempted to do that, except whoever stays here has to deal with *them*"—she indicated the three small boys—"and I think I'll be better off away from the lodge."

"Thanks for nothing," Amy called to her.

The triplets approached the desk and one of them asked, "Can we ride those horses out there?"

Amy looked at the three innocent-looking faces, and if she hadn't known what havoc they had caused the day before, she would have smiled. As it was, she hesitated

before she said, "Well, I don't know. Have any of you ever
ridden a horse before?"

"Nah," they answered in unison, and then one added,
"But we rode a dog once."

This time she did smile. "I don't think that counts. But
I'm really not the one you'll have to ask. You have to see
one of the guides about riding."

"Where are they?"

"One of the guides just left, but the other one should be
here in a few minutes. If you wait outside on the porch,
you'll see a cowboy come in. He's the one to ask."

"Okay! Come on!" they yelled to each other, and Amy
let out a sigh of relief that she had gotten them out of the
lodge without further damage. Once they were out of sight,
she forgot all about them until Derek came in.

"Did the terrible threesome ask you about riding?" she
asked him.

"You mean those triplets? No, I haven't seen them this
morning."

"They were going to wait for you on the porch. I wonder
where they went."

"Oh, they're around someplace. There aren't that many
things they can get into outside. That's what makes this a
good place for kids; it gives them a chance to run around
and let off steam after being cramped up in a city."

Amy felt he was taking another dig at her and reminded
him sharply, "We do have parks in San Francisco."

Suddenly the door burst open and the little boys came
running in. "Hey, lady, my brother's been hurt!" one of
them shouted.

Amy could see that one of the little boys was holding his
arm close to his body and there were splotches of blood on
his shirt. Before leaving the desk, she plugged in the
extension that would ring the telephone in their private
apartment. Her mother was still upstairs and would know
she was needed as soon as she answered the phone and
realized that no one was on the line.

Carefully Derek and Amy examined the boy's arm and were relieved to find only a few surface scratches.

"What happened?" Derek asked him.

"We were just playing with the kittens."

Amy gasped. "The kittens! Are they all right?"

"I don't know. I caught one of them, but he scratched me and I let him go."

"You mean you opened the cage?"

She looked around wildly for help and saw her mother coming down the stairs. "Mom, can you take care of his arm and watch the desk for me? I have to find the kittens," she said urgently. "Derek, come help me."

"Okay, but don't panic. It won't hurt them to run around for a few minutes. We'll find them," he said.

Amy and Derek had just managed to capture and pen the squealing balls of fur when they heard Maggie excitedly calling them from the front of the lodge. "Come here! Hurry!"

"I'll bet it's the triplets again," Amy said as she broke into a run.

Derek caught up with her in a single stride. "They're just little boys. They can't be at the root of everything that happens around here."

There was no need to ask anyone what the problem was. There were horses all over the parking area and in front of the lodge.

"Who opened the gate?" Derek shouted.

"I'll give you three guesses and they all end with Barnette," Amy said.

He jerked his hat off and started waving it as he began moving the horses toward the corral.

"Keep them going in that direction and I'll head them away from the road," he told Amy as he ran to block their escape.

Amy began moving her arms and shouting as she circled the horses to keep them in a tightly knit group. As she herded them from one side, Derek closed in on the other.

They kept the horses moving until they were back in the corral. Amy and Derek met at the gate.

He ran a practiced eye over the horses. "How many did Lisa take out this morning?"

"Four—five, counting her own."

"Then they're all here except Daffy." He looked around, but there was no other horse in sight. "As soon as she got out she probably headed off toward the highway. I'm tempted just to let her alone and see if she'll come back on her own."

"Are you going to do that?"

"No," he said with a sigh of resignation. "I'll chase her down the way I always do, but I want you to round up those three boys. I don't care if you have to sit on them; just make sure they're waiting on the porch steps when I get back!"

"But, Derek," Amy said, "they're just little boys."

"Amy, don't start anything with me now," he warned.

The triplets and their parents were waiting nervously for Derek when he finally returned.

"Derek," Mr. Barnette began, "I want you to know how sorry we are for what happened. If we owe anything for repairs or injuries, we're willing to make good on it."

"Yes, and we'll try to keep a closer eye on the boys. I guess they're a little high-spirited," their mother said.

Derek's manner with the parents was respectful but determined. "Thank you. No repayment is necessary, but if you and Mrs. Barnette will step inside, I'd like to speak to the boys alone."

Mrs. Barnette looked hesitantly from Derek to her husband. "Shouldn't we stay?"

"Come on, Mary. You heard what he said," her husband said as he took her arm.

Amy moved quickly to her other side and whispered, "It'll be all right. Derek has three younger brothers at home. He'll know how to handle them."

Amy stood with Mr. and Mrs. Barnette just inside the door and listened while Derek spoke.

"Well, how do you like sitting on the steps?"

"It's boring." "Not much." "They're hard," came the chorus of replies.

Derek leaned down to look them in the eyes. "All right, I'm going to make a deal with you. Every time you get into trouble, you are going to have to sit on these steps until I say you can get up, but every day that you can manage to stay out of trouble, I'll give you a riding lesson."

"Really?" one of the boys asked.

"Can we have a lesson now?"

Derek grinned. "After you help me put out the food for the horses," he said.

As Derek led the way to the barn, the little boys scrambled off the steps to follow, each one doing his best to imitate Derek's arrogant swagger.

Mr. and Mrs. Barnette smiled with relief and Amy, satisfied that Derek could handle the triplets, went back to her duties at the desk.

She watched diligently all day, looking up expectantly every time the door opened, but it was late afternoon before the Hardys finally arrived.

Amy knew them immediately. There were just two of them, a father and son. Mr. Hardy was tall; his dark hair was peppered with gray and he wore glasses. After a cursory glance at him, Amy concentrated on getting a closer look at Ray.

It was uncanny how accurately Lisa had described him. With his medium height and build, brown hair and hazel eyes, he was so average that his general description could easily fit a hundred or so boys, but Lisa hadn't left out a thing. She had described how long and thick his eyelashes were and the slight curl in his hair where it fell forward on his forehead. She had even told Amy about his nervous habit of cramming his fists into the pockets of his jeans.

Amy tried to stretch out the process of registering them as long as possible. Lisa was due to relieve her at any minute, and Amy knew she would want to see Ray. But there were no telephone calls or any other interruptions, and Mr. Hardy was so familiar with the simple registration forms that within a few minutes she had no choice but to give them their key and watch as they left to get settled in their cabin.

When the door opened again, Amy looked up expecting to see Lisa. Instead it was Ray Hardy, his fists deep in his pockets.

"Did you forget something?" she asked politely.

"Not exactly," he said. A hint of red showed through his tan as he struggled to finish. "I was just wondering . . . I mean, a girl named Lisa usually checks us in. Is she here this summer?"

"Yes, she is. In fact, I've been waiting for her to come in. I have a message for her."

"I'd be happy to take the message to her if you know where I could find her," Ray said eagerly.

Amy grabbed a sheet of notepaper and quickly scribbled, *Take your time. I'll watch the desk, Amy*. She folded it over several times and handed it to him with a smile.

"I'm sure she's in the barn. She had taken some guests fishing at Star Lake, but they got back a few minutes ago, so she must be taking care of the horses. If you'd give her that note, I'd really appreciate it."

His smile almost split his face. "I'd be happy to."

Ray was in such a hurry that he didn't see Derek coming in and almost ran into him.

Derek took one look at the matching smiles on Ray and Amy's face and immediately assumed the worst. His face clouded, but he waited until Ray was out of the lodge before saying, "I see you're up to your usual tricks."

Amy's smile died instantly. "What do you mean?"

He jerked his head in the direction that Ray had taken. "You just couldn't help flirting with him, could you?"

"For your information, all I did to make him so happy was to tell him where he could find Lisa," Amy said.

Derek's expression remained doubtful. All day, he had tried to work up enough courage to ask Amy for a date, but now, after seeing her with Ray, he couldn't tell her the real reason he had come to the lodge. Abruptly, he turned on his heel and left.

9

Amy's inevitable run-in with Derek had taken the pleasure out of discovering that Ray Hardy was interested in Lisa. Derek Jansen was, without a doubt, the most infuriating person she had ever met, she thought.

She was so angry with him for implying that she would flirt with someone that Lisa liked that she had to find some outlet for her rage. Since she couldn't leave the desk area, she began cleaning it.

She threw herself into the job with such vigor that she didn't hear the door open or see Ricky enter. She was totally oblivious to the fact that she was no longer alone until the eerie feeling of being watched came over her.

She turned around and saw Ricky leaning against the desk grinning at her.

"Ricky!" she cried, almost dropping the books she was holding, "Don't ever do that again!"

He chuckled. "I was just watching you banging things around back there and wondering what you and Derek had been fighting about this time."

Amy made a face at him and asked, "How did you know?"

"Are you kidding? You two are like fire and gasoline. You can't get near each other without setting off some kind of explosion."

"That's because he's impossible!" Amy said.

"That's funny, that's the same thing he says about you."

Amy's eyebrows shot up. "Me? I can get along with everyone around here except him. He just doesn't give me any credit for doing anything right."

Ricky shook his head. "I'm not going to get mixed up in that argument. You and Derek are going to have to work out your problems together."

"I don't think that will ever happen."

"You mean you haven't learned that the best thing about fussing and fighting is kissing and making up?"

"With Derek? Now I know you've lost your mind!"

"Oh, I don't know. I kind of thought that's what all those fireworks were leading up to."

The course of this conversation was definitely not one Amy wanted to pursue. With a look of dismay, she changed the subject.

"What are you doing here at this time of day anyway? And"—she noticed for the first time that he wasn't in his usual jeans and boots—"all dressed up?"

"That is because I just came in to see you and tell you good-bye before I leave."

"Leave? Where are you going?"

"I've been offered a job working in Ellen's father's law office in Sacramento. It will be good experience, plus I can keep it and work part time after the next college semester begins."

"I wonder if Ellen had anything to do with your getting the job?" Amy asked impishly.

"I didn't ask." He laughed.

"We're going to miss you around here," she said,

thinking how dull it would be without Ricky around. "Who's going to help James with the livestock?"

"Matt, Derek's kid brother."

"I thought he didn't want to work on the ranch."

"Neither did I, but it *is* a job and Dick pays well. At least Matt's luckier than I was. Next summer, Jason will be old enough to replace him or at least start training in Derek's spot, and Derek can work with James. I imagine Derek or Jason, or maybe both of them, will wind up managing the whole place eventually."

"Why do you make it sound as though you didn't think that would be a good idea?"

"Oh, it's not that. Derek is totally committed to the ranch, but personally, I think he's too resistant to change. If this place is ever going to compete with the other tourist spots around here, it's going to have to offer the tourists more than just scenery."

"I can't believe that someone else around here feels the same way I do! When I mentioned something about it to Derek, I thought he was going to take my head off."

Ricky reached over to ruffle her hair and said, "At least I know I'm leaving the place in good hands. You just keep working on old Derek. If anyone can turn him around, I'll bet it's going to be you."

"Don't be too sure," she said. "But you aren't leaving for good, are you?"

"Of course not. I'll be around from time to time."

He leaned across the desk and gave her a warm hug and a brief kiss on the forehead before walking jauntily out of the door. She didn't have long to sort out her feelings about his departure, for Lisa, her face glowing with happiness, was soon standing before her.

"Did you get my note?" Amy asked.

Lisa smiled widely and said, "Yes, and I checked on the mail just as you asked. Most of it's for Dad, but there's a letter in there to you from Shannon."

"Thanks," Amy said, taking the mail and putting it aside. "Well, how did it go?"

Lisa glanced around to make sure they were alone before she grabbed Amy by the shoulders.

"It was fantastic! Ray said that when he saw you behind the desk, he was afraid I wasn't going to be here this summer." Lisa rolled her eyes and gave Amy a little shake for emphasis. "You have to understand that until today, the most personal thing he's ever said to me was . . . he liked my boots! I can't believe the change in him. He even asked me to have dinner with him tonight!" She stopped suddenly and looked at Amy. "What did you do to him?"

Amy shrugged and said, "Oh, I just told him that you were crazy about him and that you were dying to see him."

"You didn't!"

Amy laughed. "Of course not, you ninny. I didn't do a thing. He asked where you were and I told him. I just sent you that note so you would know you didn't have to hurry back here to the desk."

"What am I going to wear to dinner? I don't have anything that's right."

"Look through my stuff. You can borrow anything you like."

"Thanks, and I'll take over the desk for you now. You've been back there since lunch."

"It's all right. Why don't you go ahead and start getting ready for your big evening? Considering the shape you're in, I doubt if you could even manage to put a call through. Besides, Mom will be here soon, and she can watch the desk long enough for me to change for dinner."

"Amy, I honestly don't know what I'd do without you. I need all the time I can get," Lisa said, hurrying for the stairs.

She stopped halfway up and called back softly, "Can I borrow some of your cologne too?"

"Sure, take anything you want."

The lobby seemed strangely quiet after Lisa left, and

Amy remembered that she had a letter from Shannon. She picked up the mail and began to search through it for the familiar handwriting. Somehow she knew it was going to be bad news.

"Shannon and Stephen are probably engaged by now," she said under her breath.

But it wouldn't help to put off reading the letter, so reluctantly she opened it. It was worse than she had feared. Only the fact that she couldn't leave the desk unattended and that Mrs. Avery was too busy with last-minute preparations for dinner to watch it for her kept Amy from racing up the stairs to find Lisa. Besides, it wouldn't be fair to spoil Lisa's evening with her problems. Lisa had waited too long for Ray to notice her and ask her out for Amy to take any of it away from her. She would have to keep everything to herself.

Amy soon discovered that she didn't really have to worry about hiding her distress from Lisa. Lisa was in such a fog, she wouldn't have noticed if the lodge had suddenly burned down around her. For two people who had never been close before, she and Ray certainly seemed to have a lot to talk about at dinner.

Somehow, Amy managed to get through the meal and then hurried upstairs to her room where she could be alone with her thoughts. She had to come up with a plan, and according to Shannon's letter, she didn't have much time.

After pacing the floor for the three hours it took Lisa and Ray to say good night, Amy still hadn't found a solution.

"You're still up," Lisa said as she tiptoed into the bedroom.

"Naturally," Amy said, pushing her own problem aside and focusing on Lisa. "I wanted to hear all about your evening."

"It was super! Wonderful! Fantastic!" Lisa said, dancing around the room.

"Well, light somewhere and tell me all about it."

Lisa stopped abruptly. "I'm hungry. I don't think I ate a

thing at dinner. C'mon downstairs with me, and we'll talk while we eat," she said.

"Okay. I couldn't eat at dinner myself," Amy said.

While they filled their plates and sat down at the kitchen table, Amy listened to Lisa's detailed account of her evening. When she had finished, Lisa said, "Now tell me what's bothering you."

Amy looked up guiltily. "How did you know?"

"I think it was when I said Ray proposed and that we were eloping next week and you never batted an eye," Lisa said.

"What?" Amy asked. "I know I was listening closer than that."

Lisa laughed. "I was just kidding. You responded appropriately to everything I said, but I can tell something's bothering you."

Amy sighed. "It's the letter I got from Shannon."

"What did she say? More bad news about Stephen?"

"No. In fact, she didn't even mention him." Amy took a deep breath before she continued. "Shannon's parents are coming up to Lake Tahoe for the weekend, and Shannon wants to stay with me here at the ranch."

"You don't want her to come because you're still upset about her and Stephen?" Lisa asked.

"I wish that was all there was to it." Amy groaned. "But remember all those letters I wrote to her about my wonderful new boyfriend? What am I going to do when she shows up and finds out that it was all a big lie?"

"Oh, Amy. What *are* you going to do?"

"I don't know. She's going to arrive tomorrow night unless I can come up with a good reason to keep her away."

"Do you think you can?"

"Not without a national disaster. Why can't we have an earthquake or a flood when we need it! Now everyone in San Francisco will know that I lost my boyfriend to Shannon and that I was so desperate I invented one."

"What if you got someone to pretend to be your boyfriend just for the weekend? There are a couple of cute boys staying at the ranch now. What about Bill Woodruff or Brian Warner? Wouldn't one of them do?"

Amy shook her head. "That was the first thing I thought about, but it won't work. I kept the description of my boyfriend very general so that Shannon couldn't pin me down, but I did tell her that he worked at the ranch."

"What else did you tell her?"

Amy's blush was washed out by the pale light of the single bulb.

"I know it sounds silly, but I sort of used Ricky as my model. I didn't describe him or use his name, but I told her he was mature and handsome, and I made up some stuff about how we worked together and went for long rides in the moonlight."

Lisa bit her lip. "It's too bad—I mean, this is the kind of thing Ricky would have really enjoyed. If you had asked him to pretend to be your boyfriend, he would have put on a show that would knock Shannon's eyes out, but he left today for a job in Sacramento."

"I know. He stopped by to say good-bye."

"Do you think Shannon would believe you if you said your boyfriend had just taken a job away from the ranch? I'd back up your story."

"If you had been hearing all these fantastic stories about a mysterious boyfriend who conveniently disappeared the moment you showed up, would you believe it?" Amy asked.

Lisa shook her head slowly. "No, I guess not."

For a minute the kitchen was silent as the girls were lost in thought, and then Lisa brightened.

"Amy! We can still make it work. You said you didn't use Ricky's name or his description, and there is someone else who works here."

"James is already married, so I don't think he'd be

willing to play any childish games," Amy said, her voice growing slower as she became suspicious. "And I hope you aren't going to suggest . . . Derek?"

"Why not? He'd be perfect. He works on the ranch and he's nice looking. At least, all the female guests seem to think so."

"This is supposed to be my boyfriend, remember? Derek and I can't even get along with each other for more than five minutes."

"But this is different. If he knew you needed him, he'd do it. I know he would."

Amy shook her head. "No. He's the last person I would ask to help me out of a jam like this."

"Then your only other choice is to be honest with Shannon and tell her the truth."

Amy sighed. "I know. I guess I've always known it. I just didn't want to think about it. If I hadn't tried to be so cool and had been honest with her all along, I would never have gotten myself into such a mess in the first place. I'll call her tomorrow and get it over with before she gets here. That way, at least I won't have to see her face while I'm doing it."

Amy got up and took their plates to the sink. "Come on," she said. "We'd better get to bed. Tomorrow is going to be a red-letter day for both of us."

"Did I tell you that Ray asked if we could go fishing tomorrow? Just the two of us," Lisa said as she followed Amy out of the kitchen.

"Maybe I should check to see whether the triplets would like to go with you," Amy said teasingly.

"Don't you dare!"

Once they were back in their beds, the girls had trouble getting to sleep. Lisa was already excited about seeing Ray again, and Amy was trying to figure out how to tell Shannon the truth without looking like a complete fool.

* * *

Although she tossed and turned most of the night, the next morning Amy still wasn't sure what she was going to say to Shannon, but with Shannon due to arrive that very night, she couldn't put off discussing the visit with her mother. Besides, she nursed a small hope that Maggie would have some objection to having Shannon stay with them for the weekend.

Unfortunately, Maggie was delighted with the idea. "See, I tried to tell you that you wouldn't lose your friends when we moved up here! The ranch is a perfect place to have them visit you, and since we have a few empty cabins right now, you girls can stay in one of them. What do you think?"

Amy forced a smile. "It's great, Mom. I'll call Shannon and tell her everything is set."

"Sure, go ahead, and if her mother has any doubts, let me talk to her," Maggie said.

As she dialed Shannon's number, Amy prayed for some last-minute inspiration, but her prayers didn't have time to be answered. Shannon picked up the telephone on the first ring.

"Amy?"

Amy was so surprised at the immediate response she blurted, "How did you know?"

"I've been waiting for you to call."

"I'm sorry. I didn't get your letter until yesterday afternoon, and I just finished talking to Mom. She says it's fine with her, so just tell us when we can expect you."

"Dad said we would leave as soon as he finished work today, so we should get there about eight o'clock tonight. Will you be there, or have you got a date with that boyfriend you keep bragging about?"

Amy's blood drained to her feet, making her feel lightheaded. It was obvious she wasn't going to be spared this last humiliation. "I'll be here. I shouldn't have said anything to you about my boyfriend because—"

Shannon interrupted her. "Don't you dare tell me that he's going to be away or too busy to meet me! I'm not leaving until I see him. Some of the girls said you might try to hide him somewhere while I was there so that I wouldn't steal him away."

The way you did Stephen, Amy thought. Before she could stop herself she said, "Oh, he'll be here. I'm not worried about anyone taking him away from me."

"Hey, you sound serious. Now I really can't wait to get there and meet him. In fact, I'm going to bring my camera and take some pictures of him. But speaking of bringing things, what else should I bring? Jeans? A swim suit? A dress? What?"

"How long are you going to be able to stay?"

"Unfortunately, just until Sunday morning. Dad has some kind of thing Sunday night, so we'll have to get back early."

Amy was having a hard time concentrating on the conversation. Running through her mind was the fact that she had committed herself. Now there was no backing out. She had to come up with a boyfriend by eight o'clock that night.

"Just bring some of everything," she said.

Shannon laughed. "I'll tell Mother you said that. She's already complaining that I've taken out enough outfits to stay for a week."

"Well, if things get boring, we can always have you put on a fashion show for us," Amy said and then hurried to end the conversation. "I've got to go now, but I'll see you tonight."

As soon as Shannon said good-bye and hung up, Amy began to shake. This was, without a doubt, the worst situation she had ever gotten herself into.

Lisa had left early that morning to go fishing with Ray at Star Lake, and now Amy watched anxiously for her return. When she finally saw them ride up to the barn, she went outside and waited for Lisa on the porch.

Lisa took one look at Amy's face and asked, "What happened?"

"I couldn't tell Shannon the truth."

"Oh, I see," Lisa said. "Will you let me ask Derek to help you now?"

Amy bit her lip. She knew that Derek was her only option, but still she hesitated. "What if he won't?"

"He will," Lisa insisted. "Besides, if he doesn't, I'll threaten to tell Aunt Helen about the time he tried to go ice skating on the lake and fell through the ice."

Without waiting for Amy to raise any more objections, Lisa turned around and headed for the barn, tugging Amy behind her. They found Derek inside a stall currying one of the horses.

He looked up when they came in. "I was wondering where all my help was," he said dryly. "I'm assuming that's why you came out here."

"Not exactly," Lisa said. One glance at the frozen expression on Amy's face told her that Amy wouldn't be of any help, so she forged ahead alone. "We came to ask you for a favor."

"Sure. What's up?" Derek asked offhandedly.

"Amy has a girl friend coming up for the weekend, and while she's here, we want you to pretend to be Amy's boyfriend," Lisa said bluntly.

"What!" The brush that Derek had been holding hit the floor with a noisy clatter as Derek whirled around to face them, his eyes going straight to Amy.

But she was still unable to speak, so Lisa repeated the request, this time adding, ". . . without asking any questions."

The silence in the barn stretched to an uncomfortable length, until Amy finally found her voice and managed to say, "Come on, Lisa, let's go. I knew this was a crazy idea."

"No, wait," Derek said, stopping them.

He came out of the stall, closed the gate behind him, and leaned against it. "Why me? Amy hasn't exactly been without male attention this summer. Why does she suddenly need a boyfriend?"

"It's too complicated—and personal—to explain, but will you do it?"

Derek turned to Amy and forced her to look at him. "Do you want me to?" he asked.

Amy could feel her face burning. This was worse than she had imagined, but remembering Shannon's confident insinuation, she said, "I don't have any other choice."

Derek chuckled. "Somehow I figured it must be something like that." He shrugged. "I can't see how it would hurt anyone. I guess I can," he said with elaborate casualness.

Lisa squeezed Amy's arm and then impulsively hugged Derek. "I just knew you would help."

Derek flashed a mischievous grin at Amy and held his arms open invitingly. "Don't you want to thank me too?"

Amy stepped back quickly. "Thank you very much," she said primly from a safe distance.

Derek laughed and shook his head. "You're going to have to do better than that if you hope to convince anyone that I'm your boyfriend," he said.

"I'll worry about looking convincing when Shannon gets here," Amy said, some of her old spirit returning.

"If I'm not allowed to ask any questions, who's going to tell me what I'm supposed to do?"

"Shannon won't get here until late tonight and she'll be leaving sometime Sunday morning, so it will only be a day and a half at most."

"Don't forget, Theresa's engagement party is tomorrow night."

"Yes, but we're having it at the lodge, and since we'll all be going to that anyway, no one will think anything about it if they see you there with Amy," Lisa said.

"Have you already asked someone to be your date?" Amy asked.

"No. In fact, I tried to get out of going to the thing, but Theresa threatened to get you after me if I didn't show up."

"See, it's perfect. Didn't I tell you that everything would work out?" Lisa said.

"Then that's all I have to do? Go to Theresa's party with you?" Derek asked.

"Pretty much, but it wouldn't hurt if you could manage to be pleasant when we see each other while Shannon is here."

"Pleasant? You mean, like this?"

Before she had time to react, Derek caught her arm and pulled her against him, his arms going tightly around her waist.

"What are you doing?" Amy demanded in surprise and growing anger as she struggled to loosen his grip.

"Be still," Derek said quietly.

Amy stopped struggling and looked up questioningly at him.

"Amy, if you're going to convince anyone that I'm your boyfriend, at some point you're going to have to loosen up. I just figured we might as well get the initial shock of it over with right now."

Amy recognized that there was some validity in his statement, but he needn't have surprised her like that, she thought rebelliously.

Derek continued to hold her even after she stopped struggling, but now instead of merely holding her still, his grip had loosened until his hands felt warm and comforting on her back.

Almost as if he could read her mind, Derek asked, "Now, is it so bad?"

Amy blushed. "No, I guess not," she said falteringly.

Derek grinned and released her. "I'll see you tomorrow," he said.

10

With her biggest problem solved, Amy could afford to concentrate on the other details of Shannon's visit. She was glad that her mother had suggested they use one of the empty cabins. Away from the lodge, there would be less chance of anyone overhearing any comments about the great romance between her and Derek. In spite of her nervousness about pulling the whole thing off, she couldn't help smiling when she thought about everyone's reaction to seeing her and Derek getting along with each other.

The knot in her stomach returned when she considered how difficult that was going to be. Derek had agreed to help and she didn't doubt that he would try to present as convincing a performance as possible, but she also knew that they both had volatile tempers, and there were so many things that could go wrong.

While she packed her overnight bag, Amy tried to think of every conceivable problem. She wanted to be ready with an alternate plan in case she and Derek got into one of their usual arguments. She supposed that Shannon could be there to witness the breakup of one of the world's great romances —in fact, maybe that wouldn't be such a catastrophe. It would give her a plausible reason for wanting to return to San Francisco.

Lisa came into their room and broke into her thoughts. "Do you need any help?" she asked.

"I think I have everything, but hadn't you better get busy packing your own bag?"

"I thought you and Shannon would want to be alone."

"Don't be silly," Amy said. "I want you to stay in the cabin with us. I need you to help me pull this whole thing off—that is, if you don't mind."

"Of course not. I just didn't want to butt in."

"You won't. Now hurry up and get your things packed."

After they had finished packing, the girls carried their overnight bags and the sheets and towels they would need to the cabin they were going to use. They made the beds, dusted, and straightened up, and then Lisa said, "I just remembered something."

She hurried back to the lodge. When she returned, she brought some snapshots with her. "I borrowed these from our album. I thought they might help with the charade," she said, handing Amy two pictures of Derek.

"They're the perfect touch," Amy said, taking the pictures. She tried looking at them as a stranger might. The full-length photo showed a boy of above-average height with a lean build and muscular shoulders sitting astride a horse in a confident, self-assured manner. The other, a close-up, emphasized the blueness of his eyes against his dark features, and the funny little twist of his smile made him look incredibly handsome in a mischievous, fun-loving kind of way.

It was strange that she had never noticed how good-looking Derek was. Suddenly, it struck Amy that Derek had looked just like that when he held her in the barn earlier that day. She put the pictures away, afraid to examine the feelings that they stirred. "See," she told Lisa, "I knew you would help me."

Amy would have preferred Lisa to stay with her to offer moral support until Shannon and her parents arrived, but Lisa had a date with Ray to go to a movie in Truckee and Amy couldn't begrudge her that.

The Gradys arrived while the family was having dinner, disrupting the quiet evening meal with a commotion unlike any the ranch had known before.

"Amy! We're here!" Shannon cried as she burst through the doors ahead of her parents.

Amy noticed that Shannon's dark hair had been cut in a new fashionable length. She wasn't prepared for the rush of warm feelings at seeing Shannon again. Shannon had been the one who had eased Amy's entrance into Bay View High. They had passed notes to each other in boring classes and stayed up all night studying for exams. Together they had practiced applying make-up and driving a car— sometimes simultaneously. For the moment, all thoughts of Stephen, the charade, and the pain Shannon had caused were forgotten.

Amy jumped up and ran to return the greeting and introduce Mr. and Mrs. Grady to Dick.

"This is certainly a nice place you have," Mr. Grady said to Dick.

Looking around her, Amy could see what he meant. There was an inviting fire burning in the fireplace, casting a friendly glow over everything. All the tables were occupied with people who seemed to be enjoying their food and conversation. Scattered throughout the dinner crowd were a few boys who Amy knew would attract Shannon's interest.

"Is it always like this?" Shannon whispered to Amy under the cover of their parents' conversation.

Amy grinned. "Pretty much. But you have to remember that those people are the guests. I just work here."

"Do you have to work on the weekends?"

"Usually, but not this weekend," Amy said, not bothering to explain that Helen and Theresa would be there all day Saturday preparing for the engagement party that night and that they had promised to watch the desk.

"Good. We have a lot to catch up on. Why don't we take my bags up to your room and get started?" Shannon said.

"Sure, but we're not staying in my room. Mom's letting us stay in one of the guest cabins. We'll have our own place."

"Oh, Amy, you're so lucky!" Shannon said with a lingering glance at the boys in the dining room.

After saying good-bye to Shannon's parents and separating Shannon's luggage from theirs, Shannon and Amy headed for their cabin. Purposefully, Amy led Shannon past the swimming pool, which was aglow with lights that made everything look attractive and festive.

"This is better than a country club. And to think you get to spend all summer here!" Shannon said, clearly impressed. "But do you really have to work all the time?"

"It's not that bad. Mostly, I just watch the front desk, so I get to talk to everyone who comes and goes."

"That's not work! I'd pay someone to let me sit around and talk to cute boys all day." Shannon laughed.

Amy couldn't help laughing with her. It seemed so natural to be with Shannon again. The unique part of their relationship had always been their ability to zero in on each other's wavelength.

When they reached their cabin, Shannon was the first to notice the big bunch of wildflowers wrapped in tissue paper lying in front of the door. "Is this part of the welcoming treatment?" she asked.

"Not that I know anything about," Amy said, reaching down for the flowers and seeing a card with her name on it. "They're for me," she said in surprise.

"How romantic. Who are they from?"

Amy pushed open the door and flicked on the light so that she could read the note.

Amy, it said, *Ma had us gathering flowers to decorate the lodge for Theresa's party tomorrow night, and I thought you might like these.* It was signed simply *Derek*.

"They're from Derek."

"So, that's his name! I was beginning to wonder if he had one. You know, you never mentioned it in any of your letters."

Amy laughed nervously. "Of course he has a name. Derek Jansen. I know it sounds silly, but I was afraid if I told anyone, it might jinx things."

It was the kind of explanation that Shannon could understand, and she accepted it without question. Amy breathed a sigh of relief. She had cleared the first hurdle.

Shannon indicated the flowers. "Does he do things like that very often?"

Amy's smile was genuine. "No. When you meet him tomorrow, you'll see what I mean. Derek's not exactly the flowers-and-candy kind of guy," she said. Her voice softened as she thought of him picking the flowers and leaving them for her. "But he is unpredictable."

"Then I will get to meet him?"

"Of course—what did you think?"

"Never mind, I guess it doesn't matter," Shannon said. "Do you have a picture of him?"

Giving Lisa a silent prayer of thanks, Amy produced the snapshots of Derek and handed them to her.

Shannon moved closer to the light to examine the pictures. "Amy, he's a doll! Why he's even better looking than Stephen."

Stephen's name seemed to hang in the air like a cloud over the room. Amy knew they couldn't go all weekend without mentioning him, but she wasn't ready to discuss him with Shannon. The uneasy silence was mercifully broken by the sound of the telephone. Gratefully, Amy went to answer it.

Derek's voice came over the line so clearly he might as well have been in the next room. "I was calling to see if your friend had arrived."

For Shannon's benefit, Amy gushed into the phone, "Oh Derek, I'm so glad you called."

"I take it she did and that she's in the room with you now?"

"Of course. I miss you too."

Derek laughed so loud that Amy was afraid Shannon would hear. "You know, this weekend is going to be fun. I'm going to enjoy watching you trying to be nice to me."

Amy decided to put an end to the uncomfortable conversation. "I'll see you tomorrow. Goodnight."

"Okay, I'll let you off the hook for now. Goodnight," he said and paused, his voice becoming strangely husky as he added, "sweetheart."

Before Amy could gather her thoughts, the line went dead.

Shannon had to call her twice before Amy responded. "I'm sorry, what were you saying?"

Shannon shook her head. "Brother, you have it bad! I was trying to ask you how your new sister felt about you stealing such a hunk away."

"Lisa? Oh, she's Derek's cousin, so I didn't get in her way at all. In fact, you could say she was the one who set me up with him in the first place."

"Wasn't that a lucky break! Then the two of you get along all right?"

"Better than that. I don't know what I would have done without her. You'll get to see what I mean. She's going to stay in the cabin with us this weekend."

"You mean we won't get to be alone?"

"It's all right. You'll like Lisa. She would be here now, but she had a date with one of the guests."

"I don't blame her for that. I couldn't help noticing there were some definite possibilities in the dining room," Shannon said.

It was the second time Shannon had mentioned being interested in other boys. Amy couldn't help wondering how things were going between her and Stephen, but she didn't ask because she wasn't ready to hear a detailed account of Shannon's relationship with him. Instead, she said, "Why don't we go ahead and get you unpacked?"

"Sure. I want to show you the new outfit I got for this weekend. I found this fantastic little shop on Jackson Street."

For the next few hours, Shannon and Amy drifted effortlessly into their old pattern of easy give-and-take. There was a lot of news about the old crowd back home for Amy to catch up on, and by avoiding any mention of Stephen, they gossiped nonstop until Lisa returned home from her date.

Amy made the introductions. After only a few minutes of stilted, polite conversation, the girls relaxed.

"Do you know what we forgot to bring here with us?" Lisa asked casually.

Amy had already thought of it. "Yes. We didn't bring any food."

"Shall we take Shannon on a raid of the kitchen?"

"How are we going to get in? It's not as if we were in our own bedroom."

Lisa grinned and held up a key. "The back door. I got it when I went by to let Dad and Maggie know I was home."

"Great." Amy smiled. "Come on, Shannon."

The three girls crept across the grounds and through the back door of the lodge. They gathered up all the food they could carry and took it back to their cabin. As they spread the food out on the table, Shannon said in mock complaint, "You two make me so jealous. You must have so much fun together."

"Yes, we do," Amy admitted. It was funny that it took someone like Shannon to make her realize just how many things about the ranch and Lisa she really liked.

It was long after midnight before the girls settled down to sleep. When they did, they almost overslept and were later than usual going to breakfast the next morning. If Lisa and Amy hadn't joined forces to hurry Shannon along, they might have missed it altogether.

"You look fine. Come on or there won't be any food left," they said, urging her on.

"Just let me put on a little mascara. I want to look nice in case I meet Amy's boyfriend."

"Derek's probably already left on a trail ride. He may not be back until lunch," Amy said.

Unfortunately, Derek was standing in front of the corral as though he waited there for Amy every morning. As soon as he saw the girls come out of the cabin, he called to them and started over.

Exchanging a quick glance with Lisa, Amy put on a big smile and changed her direction, heading toward Derek.

He met them halfway, and as if it were the most natural thing in the world for him to do, he draped his arm around Amy's shoulders and gave her a brief, possessive hug. "I was beginning to think you weren't going to come out today," he chided her.

"We stayed up talking all night," Amy said ruefully, giving him what she hoped was a believable adoring look. "Derek, this is my friend, Shannon Grady."

Derek extended his hand. "It's nice to meet you, Shannon."

"Thank you," Shannon said. "Amy's told me so much about you, I've been dying to meet you."

"Really?" The corners of his mouth deepened in amusement, and his fingers tugged at the loose curls at Amy's neck. "What have you been saying about me?"

Amy reached up to trap his fingers in her hand. It was hard enough for her to concentrate with him so close; she didn't need the added havoc that his hand was causing. "Nothing but the truth," she said before asking, "Why haven't you left on a trail ride?"

"I was stalling to see if you and the other girls would like to come with us."

"I can't," Lisa spoke up. "I've already made plans."

"What about it, Shannon? Would you like to go?"

"You know I've never ridden a horse before," Shannon said, looking at Amy.

"You can ride Lady," Amy and Derek said simultaneously and laughed because they had had the same thought.

"Really, Shannon, you should go with them. Lady is so gentle, all you have to do is sit on her," Lisa added.

"Okay, if you all think I should. I guess I'm game enough to try anything once."

"Go ahead and have breakfast, and I'll have the horses ready as soon as you get through," Derek said.

When Amy would have walked away with Lisa and Shannon, Derek held her back. "I want to talk to you for a minute."

Shannon glanced back at them archly but allowed Lisa to lead her away.

Amy waited until they were on the porch before looking questioningly at Derek, who was still watching Shannon and Lisa.

"Your friend is a pretty girl," he said.

"Are you sorry that you agreed to pretend to be my boyfriend while she's here?" she asked, somewhat miffed.

"I didn't say that. I was just being pleasant."

"I'm sorry," she said immediately, feeling embarrassed. "I guess I'm just nervous. Actually, you've been great."

His eyes were twinkling with amusement. "You know, that's the first time you've ever apologized to me."

"Well, you haven't ever apologized to me, and sometimes you've been just as wrong."

"I guess you're right. Maybe we can both learn something this weekend."

His voice was sincere, and the warmth in his eyes made Amy blush. With a great effort, she broke the tension by asking, "What did you want?"

"If Shannon rides Lady, I'm going to have to give you another horse. Is there any particular one you'd like?"

Amy looked toward the corral and bit her lip. "Not really. Any one that you think I can handle will be all right."

He nodded and said, "Okay. Go on and hurry up Shannon."

Lisa and Shannon had already fixed Amy a plate, and as she slid into the space between them, she leaned over to Lisa and whispered, "Why aren't you coming with us?"

"Ray didn't sign up, and I thought I would just hang around here and see what he had in mind," Lisa whispered back.

Amy turned her attention to her breakfast. She and Shannon finished as quickly as possible and then hurried back to the corral, where Derek was waiting with the other riders.

Amy saw that he had chosen the sleek, high-spirited Daffy for her to ride. "Are you sure I can handle her?"

"I wouldn't let you try if I didn't think you could," Derek said as he cupped his hands for her foot and boosted her into the saddle.

Checking the fit of her stirrups, he gave her some last-minute instructions. "In some ways, you're going to find her easier to ride than Lady, but you will have to use your knees more to control her, and don't let the reins get slack for a second. She'll be fine as long as she knows you're in charge."

Dick had led Lady to the mounting block and was helping Shannon get settled.

"My goodness, she's so high! Are you sure she's not going to buck me off?" Shannon said nervously.

Amy and Derek couldn't help laughing at the idea of Lady bucking.

"Was I like that?" Amy asked.

Derek grinned, "Just like that."

Amy nudged Daffy closer to Lady, immediately appreciating Daffy's quick response. "Shannon, I'll be riding up front with Derek. We'd be happy to have you ride beside us, but Lady always follows the other horses. I learned to ride on her and believe me, she's unflappable. Just sit still and enjoy the scenery."

"I'll keep an eye on her," Bill Woodruff, who was also part of the group, volunteered.

A last glance at Shannon told Amy that she was happy to have the attention of one of the male guests, so Amy waved and moved up to join Derek at the head of the small group.

As they passed through the gates, another horse shouldered Daffy, causing her to brush against the fence. Immediately, she reared and started to bolt forward. Automatically, Amy brought her up sharply.

Derek pulled up his horse and waited until Amy had Daffy under control again. "Are you all right?" he asked with concern.

Amy's face was flushed but proud. "I'm fine."

She was rewarded with an approving smile. "Good girl."

For a while the narrow trail forced them to ride single file, but when it widened again, Amy brought Daffy up beside Derek. "She really is wonderful to ride. I don't mean to sound disloyal to Lady, but this gives you a whole new feeling about riding."

Derek nodded and then frowned. "That's the problem with her. If she wasn't so good in other ways, I would have already sold her."

"Sell her? You can't mean that!"

"What if she had pulled the stunt she did with you with some kid on her back? No, if we can't trust her with the guests, she isn't earning her keep."

"I'll ride her. After today, I don't think I want to go back to riding Lady."

Derek gave her a strange look. "What if I agree to keep her as long as you stay?"

It was a second before Amy realized that she had been

trapped, and when she did, her eyes flashed angrily at him. "You know I'm planning to go back to San Francisco."

"That's what I mean."

"That's not fair!"

"Hadn't you better watch your temper? You wouldn't want Shannon to think we were arguing, would you?"

Amy glanced behind them to see whether Shannon had detected anything, but she was talking to Bill and seemed blithely unaware of them. Keeping her face and voice carefully controlled, Amy said, "We'll pick up this discussion after Shannon leaves."

Derek laughed, his good humor restored. "I wouldn't be at all surprised," he said before becoming serious again. "Observation Rock is just ahead. That's probably as far as your friend should ride on her first day out."

"Yes, I don't want her to be too sore to enjoy the party tonight."

"I know she'll be all right going back on Lady, but how do you feel about riding back with Daffy?"

"Perfectly safe," she assured him.

"I told Dick I would send you and Shannon back alone, so he'll be watching for you. Don't leave the trail for any reason, because if you're not back soon he'll come looking for you."

With a nod of understanding, Amy pulled Daffy out of line and waited for the other horses to pass and Shannon to catch up with her.

11

Do you want to go back to the ranch?" Amy asked.

Shannon looked toward the other riders. "Where are they going?"

"About another ten or fifteen miles straight up into the mountains," Amy said. "They'll be gone for a couple of hours."

Shannon made her decision quickly. "Oh, yes, I think I'm ready to go back now. How do you turn this animal around?"

Amy grinned. "I'll show you."

She brought Daffy across the trail in front of Lady and began heading back down the trail. For a moment Lady seemed to consider her choices of following the main group of horses or falling in behind Daffy and going back to the corral. She opted for the corral.

"Hey, how did you know she would do that?" Shannon asked in amazement.

Amy smiled, "You pick up a few things. Besides, Lady

131

isn't fond of long trips. Her favorite trail is the one that heads back toward the barn.''

When they got back to the corral, Shannon refused to dismount until Amy took a picture of her on Lady. ''Listen, she said, ''no one is going to believe I rode a horse unless I bring home some proof.''

Once that was done, they went to look for Lisa. She wasn't in their cabin, the barn, or anywhere around the corral, so Amy suggested they check the lodge.

When she opened the door, her eyes widened in surprise and she looked around in amazement. The dining room chairs had been stacked on the tables and all the other furniture was pushed to one corner of the room. There were people Amy had never seen before, scurrying around the lodge.

''What in the world—'' she asked as her mother approached them.

''We're just getting everything ready for the party tonight. We removed the rugs and are having the floor waxed for dancing, and we're trying to see if we can set up the band on the stairs.''

''A party? Dancing? That sounds like fun. Are we invited too?'' Shannon asked.

''Certainly. Everyone is. It's an engagement party for Theresa Jansen, Dick's niece,'' Maggie explained. ''All of the family's friends and, since it's being held here, all the ranch guests are invited.''

Amy saw Helen and Theresa across the room and waved to them. ''Is everything going to be ready in time?'' she asked her mother.

''Sure. You won't recognize this place by tonight.''

''What about meals today? Where are the guests going to eat?''

''Outside. Dick's barbecuing, and he's set up picnic tables out there. I've got to get back to work. Did you girls need anything?''

''We're looking for Lisa. Have you seen her?''

"Not lately. She and Ray were on the porch for awhile, but they must have gone for a walk. Was it important?"

"No, we just wanted to see if she wanted to join us for a swim. If you see her, tell her where we are," Amy said as she and Shannon left to get their suits.

The morning sun hadn't taken the chill off the water, and their swim proved to be more invigorating than relaxing. After a few laps, the girls spread their towels out on the deck so they could stretch out and let the sun warm them.

Lying only a few feet away, Shannon studied her friend. "You know, Amy, you've changed this summer."

"Really? How?"

"I can't put my finger on it—you just seem so together. I never would have thought you would fit in on a ranch, but you do."

Amy shrugged. "I guess I have adjusted, and it really wasn't all that difficult. The people here are nice, and having to pitch in and help just naturally makes you feel like a part of things."

"Yes, but it's something else too. I was watching you and Derek this morning."

Amy's heart caught in her chest. Had Shannon noticed them arguing? "What about it?"

"You look so perfect together, as though you were made for each other. I'm really envious of you."

Amy couldn't help smiling in relief. In fact, things were going so well it didn't even hurt her to bring up Stephen's name. "Me? What about you? You're dating Stephen Kemp and he's not exactly small time."

"I suppose so," Shannon admitted uneasily. "I felt pretty good about dating him until I saw you and Derek together. Now I know it's not the same. You two are so natural and comfortable with each other. Do you know that one day when I was shopping at the mall, I saw Stephen and I actually hid from him because I had a pimple and I was afraid he would notice it?" She laughed.

"My relationship with Derek is different," Amy said,

trying to explain without divulging that there really was no romance. "We spend a lot of time with each other every day. It's not like just seeing him for a few hours on a date."

"Do you ever fight?" Shannon asked.

Amy let out her breath in a gasp that ended with a giggle. "Are you kidding? All the time! Why?"

"I've never argued with Stephen. I wouldn't dream of disagreeing with him—not out loud anyway."

Amy knew exactly what she meant. She had done the same thing when she dated Stephen, but she couldn't imagine doing that now, and certainly not with Derek. "We're two completely different people. You can't expect us to agree on everything."

"Well, you're obviously doing something right," Shannon said. "Derek seems to be crazy about you."

Amy rolled over onto her back, facing the sun and giving herself a plausible excuse for closing her eyes before Shannon could see the truth in them. One day, when this was all behind them, she'd tell Shannon the whole story, and they would laugh at how well Derek had played his part.

Shannon interrupted her thoughts. "Amy, what are you going to do when the summer's over? Are you still planning to come back to San Francisco?"

"I don't know."

Amy knew Shannon would attribute her indecision to Derek, but it was much more than that. It seemed that she had spent all summer waiting and planning for the day she could return and begin her campaign to get Stephen back, but she was beginning to have second thoughts. Did she really want him? What would it do to her friendship with Shannon? She would need some answers before she reached any decision.

Suddenly she asked, "Are you going steady with Stephen?"

"Why? Are you thinking about dumping Derek and

going back to him?'' Shannon asked. She turned to face
Amy, but Amy kept her face toward the sun and her eyes
closed.

Shannon had come so close to what Amy had been
thinking that she was forced to deny it stridently. ''No, of
course not! I was thinking about the party tonight. Since it
is an engagement party for Derek's sister, we have to be
there, but I didn't arrange a date for you because I wasn't
sure how serious things were between you and Stephen. I
hope you'll want to go anyway.''

''I do. That boy who was riding beside me this morning,
Bill something-or-other, mentioned the party this morning
and asked me to save him a dance. I was hoping we were
going, and don't worry, it won't affect my relationship with
Stephen.''

With her eyes still closed, Amy's sense of hearing was
more sensitive than usual and she picked up the sound of a
light footstep. She squinted through her lashes just in time
to see Lisa standing over her with a pail of water.

''No! Don't!'' She squealed, rolling away as the cold
water splashed over her.

''I'm sorry, I couldn't resist.'' Lisa laughed as she
plopped down beside Amy.

Amy picked up a towel to dry herself and asked, ''Where
have you been all day? We looked for you.''

Lisa shrugged. ''Around. Ray and I started walking and
ended up at one of the cow pastures.''

''That must be five miles away!''

''I know. Thank heavens we ran into James. We rode
around with him for awhile, and then he brought us back in
his pickup.''

''Who's James?'' Shannon asked.

Lisa grinned. ''Another cousin, but he's grown, married,
and has a kid.''

''Oh,'' Shannon said, losing interest.

''Now Ray's gone fishing with his father—but he asked
me to be his date at the party tonight.''

"I'd say that's pretty good. He's been here three days, and so far you've had three dates," Amy said.

"What about you, Shannon? Do you want us to fix you up with a date or would you rather go stag?"

"I don't know. Bill said something about saving him some dances."

"And Brian Warner asked me about you this morning after breakfast," Lisa said. "Or I could introduce you to some of the local boys. There will be plenty of them at the party too."

"With that many boys, I think I'd rather go stag," Shannon said and then lay back on her towel and stretched her arms wide. "Oh, I just love this place!"

The girls spent most of the afternoon getting ready for the party. They washed, rolled, tweezed, filed, and shaved until there wasn't one follicle or appendage that hadn't been polished, curled, or shaped.

"You know," Lisa said, seeing the amount of powder, perfumes, creams, and lotions scattered around the room, "we have enough stuff in here to open a store."

"Yes, and since there's a blonde, brunette, and I guess Lisa could be called a redhead, there isn't a single shade of makeup that's missing," Shannon said with a laugh.

"I just think it was awfully nice of Theresa to have this party so we could all have a chance to get dressed up," Amy said.

Even though they laughed and joked as they dressed, each girl, for reasons of her own, took pains with her appearance. Lisa wore a yellow sundress that brought out the red highlights in her deep brown hair, and Shannon had chosen a flowered red dress that set off her dramatic dark coloring.

Amy had decided on a completely different look for herself. With Shannon's help and expert use of the curling iron, she had styled her hair so that one side fell forward to shade part of her face and the other was held back by a spray of baby rosebuds and white baby's breath. Her off-the-shoulder dress was the same rosy shade of pink as the flowers and set off the creamy, sun-blushed tone of her skin. She took infinite care with her makeup, using mascara to darken and lengthen her lashes and adding a touch of gray eye shadow to create a more dramatic look.

Lisa and Shannon had voiced their opinion of her appearance before they left, but it was the warmth and approval in Derek's eyes that made the extra time and trouble she had gone to worthwhile.

"You look beautiful," he said softly when she opened the door at his knock.

Sternly, she ordered her pulse to stop racing. "Thank you. Shall we go?" She swallowed nervously, not able to take her eyes away from Derek in his dark suit and crisp white shirt.

"Have Lisa and Shannon already gone?"

Now she understood why he had paid her the compliment. It was just part of the game they were playing. "Yes. Ray came by for Lisa, and Shannon walked over with them," she said, trying not to sound disappointed.

In the darkness, as they walked toward the lodge Derek reached for her hand as naturally as if he had always done so. "How's it going?"

"What?" Amy asked. She was having a hard time concentrating on anything but the feel of his hand, warm and steady, on hers.

"This whole play-acting thing you're pulling on Shannon? Is she buying it?"

"So far. She'll be leaving before noon tomorrow. Do you think we can stay civil with each other until then?"

His smile was a flash of white teeth in the darkness. "If you keep wearing that perfume, our truce could last forever."

Confused by the turn of the conversation, Amy looked around for something else to talk about that would put them back on safer ground. "Goodness, I knew they were expecting a crowd, but I never thought there would be this many people."

The parking lot was filled with cars. Light, music, and laughter seemed to spill out of the lodge as they made their way up the steps. Inside, the plain, almost spartan, lodge had been transformed into a riot of color with wild flowers and candles.

"Theresa must be in her glory about now," Derek said wryly as he looked around. "Shall we try to make our way through this mob and find her? If I don't, she'll swear I didn't show up."

"Yes. I want to meet her fiancé," Amy said.

Slowly but steadily, Derek made a path for them through the crowd of well-wishers that surrounded Theresa and Dennis George, her fiancé. After giving his sister a hug and shaking hands with Dennis, Derek introduced Amy.

"So you're the one who's keeping Derek in line these days," Dennis said in a teasing voice.

"I don't think anyone could do that," Amy returned, "but it doesn't keep me from trying."

"And trying, and trying, and trying," Derek added with a feigned grimace.

Dennis laughed as he slapped Derek on the back. "You'd better watch out, pal. When a girl starts trying to change you, she can be dangerous."

As someone else moved up to speak to the engaged couple, Derek and Amy found themselves crowded away.

Even though they were surrounded by people, Amy felt she was alone with Derek, and it wasn't an altogether unpleasant experience. She broke the silence that had sprung up between them by asking, "Do you see Lisa or Shannon anywhere?"

"No, but they could be on the other side of the room. Why don't we get out on the dance floor and move around? Maybe we can spot them."

"Okay, but . . ."

Derek was already leading her to the dance floor, and as he gathered her into his arms, he asked, "What?"

"I was just going to say that if there was someone else you wanted to dance with, it would be all right. I don't expect you to stay with me every minute."

She felt rather than saw him smile. "Don't worry about me," he said, his voice warm and husky in her ear. "I'm doing just fine."

The next day, this courteous and considerate stranger would be wearing jeans and boots and more than likely arguing with her about something, but that was in the future. For the present, she would follow his lead and just relax and enjoy the party. She and Derek knew each other so well that it was almost like being with a good friend, only better. Much better.

Every now and then, Amy would catch a glimpse of Shannon or Lisa in the crowd, but it wasn't until hours later, when the crowd had thinned out a bit, that she and Derek ran into them at the refreshment table.

"Are you having a good time? I hope you haven't felt neglected." Amy said to Shannon.

Shannon smiled. "Not at all. I'm having a wonderful time. I've met some of the local boys, and Bill Woodruff asked whether he could walk me back to our cabin."

"Hey, you guys," Lisa said, interrupting them. "They're going to start square dancing. Come on!"

Derek reached for Amy's hand, but she pulled back. "I don't know how."

"It's easy," he assured her. "Just watch everyone else and besides, the caller will tell you what to do."

Actually, Amy discovered, square dancing was more complicated than Derek had made it seem. It was a strenuous, fast-paced dance, and unless you understood the terminology, the caller's instructions were of no help whatsoever.

But gamely she kept twisting and turning in whatever

direction she was pointed until the dance ended and she found herself on the opposite side of the room with neither Derek nor Lisa anywhere in sight.

Someone grabbed her from behind, and Amy turned with a startled jerk.

"Ricky! I didn't know you'd be here!" she cried with pleasure.

"Sure." He smiled. "If I had missed this shindig, Theresa would have had me ostracized."

"I'm glad you came. We've missed you."

"I couldn't help noticing that there have been some changes around here. Are my eyes deceiving me, or have you and Derek decided to take my advice and start kissing instead of fighting?"

Amy blushed. "Not exactly. We just called a truce for the weekend. Before tomorrow is over, we'll probably be fighting again."

"Oh, you never can tell what these truces might bring," he said, teasing her. "By the way, who was that cute girl in the red dress I saw you talking to?"

"Shannon Grady. She's a friend of mine from San Francisco."

Ricky's face fell. "A friend of yours? Then she must be about . . ."

"Sixteen," Amy supplied.

"I was afraid of that," he said and then brightened. "Just be sure to invite her back in a few years."

"Ricky, you're incorrigible!"

"Yeah, aren't I though?" he said agreeably.

"There you are," Derek said to Amy as he joined them. Then he turned to greet his cousin. "Hello, cuz, how are things in the legal world?"

"Just fine," Ricky said, taking note of the arm Derek had slipped around Amy's waist. "Since you have things well in hand here, I'd better go find my date before she leaves with someone else."

As Ricky walked away, Derek asked, "What happened to you?"

"I don't know. When the caller said 'Allemande left,' I think I must have 'do-si-doed.' The next thing I knew, I was in an entirely different group and I just kept getting passed from one partner to the next."

Derek grinned. "That can happen. Do you want to try it again, or would you rather sneak outside for some fresh air?"

"Some air, I think. I'm not going to try square dancing again until I have some lessons."

Once outside, Amy took a deep breath. "Hmmm. It feels good out here."

"Yeah, it was getting a bit stuffy in there," Derek said, loosening his tie.

As if by mutual consent, they stopped walking and stood at the edge of the pool of light that was coming from the open door.

"Everyone seems to be having a good time, especially your friend," Derek commented.

"Yes, but I'm afraid she's going to leave with the wrong impression of the ranch. She'll think we do things like this all the time."

"Why are you concerned about that? After all, it was your plan that she get the wrong impression about us."

"That's different."

"How?"

"It just is," Amy insisted. She didn't want to be reminded that that was the only reason Derek was being nice to her. "Maybe we should go back inside."

He seemed totally relaxed, and before Amy was aware of his intentions, Derek's hand moved forward, capturing her arm and preventing any escape. "Not yet. I want to talk. Does it have something to do with a guy?"

"You weren't supposed to ask any questions," Amy said.

"I never agreed to that," Derek said. "It's my guess that Shannon stole your boyfriend and you are using me to show her that you don't care."

Without thinking, Amy blurted, "She did not! I moved away. He never paid her any attention until after I left."

While he had been talking, Derek had inched his hands up her arms to her shoulders, forcing her to remain facing him when she would have turned away.

"So that was it. And I'm being used to soothe your ego and maybe to make the other guy jealous," he said, lowering his voice and moving closer to her. "And this guy, whoever he is, is the main reason you want to return to San Francisco, isn't he?"

Derek's face was now only inches from hers, and Amy was having a difficult time trying to sort out her thoughts. She had seen a different side of Derek, one to which she was very attracted. "I don't know," she said lamely.

Almost as though he had read her mind, Derek began moving his thumbs in little circles on her shoulders, sending shivers up her arms. He had moved closer so slowly that it had been imperceptible, but when he lowered his head to her, Amy tried to step back.

She didn't want this to happen now—not while she was still confused. She needed time to think. "Derek . . ."

"Shhh," he whispered, his mouth close to her ear. "Your friend is standing at the door watching us."

Lightly, he kissed her temple. "Wouldn't she expect us to be doing something like this if we happened to find ourselves alone in the dark?" he asked softly, with a hint of laughter, as he planted more light, teasing kisses on her neck before moving back to the sensitive spot near her ear.

"I guess so," she said with difficulty, trying to force herself to relax. Instinctively, she had raised her hands to ward off any more kisses, and now she let them slide up to the top of his shoulder. She hoped Shannon would leave soon. This had to stop!

"Is she still there?" she asked desperately as Derek kissed her on her cheek.

"Uh-huh," he murmured.

Now his lips were closing in on hers, and suddenly Amy didn't care whether Shannon was watching or not. She forgot everyone and everything except Derek.

Amy was lost in the heady world of his kiss when she heard someone call her name.

"Amy? Are you out here?"

Startled, she jerked away from Derek and then let out a sigh of relief when Lisa appeared. "You scared me to death. We thought it was Shannon."

"Oh, don't worry about her. She and Jim left right after the square dancing started," Lisa said.

Amy whirled on Derek. "You said she was watching us!"

Derek shrugged. "I figured it was worth a try."

Color flooded Amy's face as she tried to think of something bad enough to call him. "You . . . you . . ."

Derek interrupted her. "What's making you so angry? That I tricked you, or that you forgot your precious boyfriend?"

"I was just pretending and you know it!"

Derek shook his head. "It may have started off that way, but that wasn't how it ended. You weren't pretending all the time," he said confidently, "and neither was I."

Before Amy had time to grasp the meaning of what he'd said, Derek disappeared into the darkness. She stood there for a minute longer, half hoping he would return. When he didn't, she fell into step with Lisa and headed back toward their cabin.

12

It was after nine o'clock before the girls stirred the next morning. The hour wasn't late for Shannon, but Lisa and Amy were accustomed to rising early, and they moved around the cabin feeling sluggish and lazy.

Lisa stretched. "Instead of all of us getting dressed and going over to eat in the dining room, why don't I slip over and bring something back from the kitchen?"

"That would be great," Amy said. "And while Shannon packs, I'll start stripping the cabin so it will be ready for the next guests."

As Lisa left, Shannon sat up in the middle of her bed and hugged her knees to her chest. "I've had such a good time, I hate to think about going home," she said.

"I'm going to miss you," Amy said.

"But not too much. At least you'll still have Derek."

The mention of Derek's name almost destroyed Amy's composure. After all that had happened the night before, she wasn't sure she would ever be able to face him again, but that wasn't her only problem.

Her plan had worked. She knew that Shannon was totally convinced that Derek was her boyfriend, but instead of the elation she had expected, Amy felt uncomfortable and shabby. She sat down on the side of the bed next to Shannon.

"Please don't hate me, but there's something I have to tell you before you leave."

Amy looked so serious that Shannon sat up straighter and leaned forward. "What?"

"It's about Derek. He's not my boyfriend . . . and he never was."

There was a moment of stunned silence before Shannon said, "I don't believe it! What about the dance last night, the flowers, and all of those secret smiles and looks between the two of you?"

"It was all an act. I was so jealous of you for taking Stephen away from me, that I asked Derek to pretend to be my boyfriend while you were here."

"You mean there was never anyone else?"

Amy shook her head. "No."

"Then why didn't you answer any of Stephen's letters?"

Now it was Amy's turn to be confused. "What letters? I haven't heard a thing from him since I left San Francisco."

"Oh, no! Oh, Amy!" Shannon buried her face in her hands. "You must have thought I was terrible! I can't believe Stephen told such an awful lie!"

"What did he say?"

"It started right after you left. The day after Jeannette's party, he called me. I didn't think anything about it at first because we just spoke briefly at the party, and I thought he wanted to ask me some more about how you were doing and that sort of thing. But he asked me for a date. I turned him down, and I told him that I couldn't date anyone you liked."

Shannon crawled off the bed and began pacing the floor in agitation while she told the rest of the story.

"The next day, or the day after—I'm so confused now I

may not have it all straight—he started showing up everywhere I went, at the tennis club, at parties; he even came by my house to see me almost every day. To be honest, I liked the attention, but I wouldn't date him. He told me he had written you every day and that you wouldn't answer his letters or return his phone calls."

"I wrote him! You know I did. You even mentioned it in one of your letters."

"Yes. I wanted to see if you'd tell me the same thing he said you told him—that you were coming back but you weren't going to date him anymore. Remember, you called me after you got my letter and told me—"

"That I was seeing someone else," Amy finished for her. "I can't believe I played right into Stephen's hands."

"Yes, but I wanted to believe it," Shannon said, accepting some of the blame. "And as soon as you said it was all right, I started dating him."

"If I had been honest with you, none of this would have happened. I'm sorry, but don't be upset about it. It really and truly doesn't matter any more. I honestly don't care about Stephen, and considering what he did to get you, he must really like you. So, in a strange way, everything has worked out."

Shannon's face fell. "No. I haven't told you the whole story."

"Oh, no—what now?"

"Stephen's dropped me, or at least I think he has. I haven't heard from him or seen him in over a week. I don't know what happened. Everything was wonderful between us. We enjoyed the same things, and we never disagreed, but then he started showing up late for dates and a few times he stood me up altogether. And now this disappearing act. I don't know what went wrong."

"I think I do," Amy said. "Don't you see, Shannon? When you wouldn't go out with him, he chased you. But as soon as he knew he had you, he didn't care anymore. It wasn't anything you did. That's just the way he is. To

Stephen everything is a game; he's not honest with himself or with anyone else. I know, because that's how I caught him in the first place, and the awful thing is that I was becoming just like him. We're both lucky to be out of his trap."

"You know what I can't believe? How close he came to breaking up the best friendship I've ever had. We can't let anyone come between us again."

"Agreed," Amy said as they solemnly shook hands on the pact.

Shannon suddenly brightened. "You know what else this means? Since there's nothing between you and Derek, there's no reason for you to stay here."

"Mom's still here, and Dick and Lisa."

"Yes, but they'll be here next summer, and you can still come up to see them on weekends and holidays. Please say you'll come back! I've missed you so much this summer and now that I've lost Stephen, I really need you. It isn't the same with Lisa. I mean, she's never been in school with you so she won't miss you the way I will. And you know, I'll bet we could come up with some sort of scheme to get back at Stephen Kemp. We could teach him a lesson he'd never forget!"

Amy grinned. "I have to admit, that's a tempting idea."

"Your mother and Dick *will* let you come back? You didn't make that up, did you?"

"No. They said it was up to me."

"Oh, it's going to be wonderful! And next summer, we can come back here together."

They were interrupted by a loud knock at the door. "Hey, open up in there. This stuff is heavy," Lisa called.

Amy signaled Shannon not to say anything more before she opened the door for Lisa.

Lisa maneuvered a large tray through the door and placed it on the table. "Shannon," she said, "Maggie said your parents have already called and they're on their way."

"Oh, rats!" Shannon said, grabbing the outfit she had planned to wear home and disappearing into the bathroom.

When she had closed the door behind her, Lisa asked Amy, "Are you all right? You look a little funny."

"No, everything's fine. I told Shannon the truth about Derek and me."

"How did she take it?"

"Pretty well, and I found out something too. Shannon didn't do anything behind my back. Stephen was lying to both of us."

While they talked, Lisa and Amy had cleared off the small table and as soon as Shannon was dressed, they sat down and had their breakfast. When they had finished, they gathered all their things and the dirty linens and took them back to the lodge, just minutes before Mr. and Mrs. Grady arrived.

Mr. Grady seemed even more impressed with the ranch now that he was seeing it in daylight. "If I didn't have to get back home so early, I'd like to take a tour of your place," he told Dick. "Maybe next summer we can come up and spend some time here. I know Shannon would like that."

"We'd love to have you, but you don't have to wait until next year. Officially we don't operate the guest facilities all year round, but friends are welcome anytime," Dick said.

"Thank you. We just might take you up on that offer," Mr. Grady said, to the girls' smiling approval.

"See," Shannon whispered to Amy, "we can come back anytime you want to, and by going to school in San Francisco and spending the holidays and vacations here, you'll have the best of both worlds."

The arrangement sounded feasible and Amy said, "Give me a chance to talk to Mom and Dick. I'll call you in a few days."

"Okay, but don't wait too long," Shannon said as she crawled into the back seat of the car.

Amy watched the Grady's car until it was only a streak of

dust in the distance. She felt as if one end of her heart was hooked to the back of the car and the other was tied to the ranch and between them, she was being pulled apart.

Shannon's suggestion that she divide her time between the two places sounded great in theory, but Amy knew that she couldn't spend the rest of her life in limbo. Eventually, she would have to commit herself to one place.

Amy turned and saw that Lisa and her mother had gone inside the lodge. Only Dick was standing on the porch, watching her.

"Are you all right?" he asked.

Amy nodded. "Just confused."

"If it means that much to you, you know that we won't force you to stay here."

"Yes, I know, but I almost wish someone would tell me what to do. Any decision I make is going to hurt someone."

Dick came down from the porch and put his arm around her shoulders. "You may not want to hear this right now, but you've just learned an important lesson about growing up. For the rest of your life, you're going to have to make decisions that won't have just one right answer. Sometimes you'll just have to decide what's right for you. Why don't you think about it a little longer? There are still a few weeks before school starts."

"But it seems as though I've spent all summer with this hanging over my head. I want to get it settled and get on with my life," she said. "Do you think anyone would mind if I went off by myself for awhile?"

"No, take all the time you need," Dick said.

There was no place near the lodge where she could go to think and know that she wouldn't be disturbed, but there was no reason she couldn't saddle up Lady and go for a ride by herself.

When Amy reached the corral, she changed her mind. What she needed was a brisk ride, a real workout, not some slow, plodding walk.

"Sorry, Lady," she said to the sleepy-looking horse, "I guess even I've outgrown you."

Lady didn't seem to mind and simply moved aside as Amy reached for Daffy's bridle. Aware of Daffy's skittish personality, Amy tied her securely to the fence while she got the saddle. She had no difficulty saddling Daffy and, feeling confident and independent, she rode off toward Observation Rock.

As she climbed into the hills, putting some distance between herself and the ranch, she began to think more clearly.

Shannon had been a loyal friend even when she had doubted her. Didn't Amy owe her something? But was that her only reason for returning to San Francisco? Dick and Lisa had become part of her family. They had accepted her into their lives knowing she might leave. Did she owe them more than she owed Shannon?

She pulled Daffy to a stop when they came to the clearing in front of the large, jutting rock and looked down at the ranch spread out below her. It was such a picturesque scene, she thought, that if she could just scoop the whole thing in her arms and carry it with her wherever she went, all her problems could be solved.

Her thoughts were interrupted by a rustle in the underbrush, and suddenly a little rabbit, not much bigger than a ground squirrel, ran out from the bushes.

Instinctively Amy knew what he was going to do, and she tried to tighten her grip on the reins and grab the saddle horn. But her reaction time was too slow.

The rabbit dashed between Daffy's legs and the horse reared in fright.

Amy felt herself begin to slip. Desperately, she tried to clasp the horse with her knees, but she hadn't tightened the saddle securely and it slipped—just enough for her to lose her balance.

Knowing that she was going to fall, Amy kicked her feet

out of the stirrups, let go of the reins, and tucked her arms around her head, mentally reminding herself to roll away as soon as she touched the ground, for the biggest danger was from the powerful hooves that could come down on her.

She had never fallen from such a height before and was unprepared for the impact. For a moment she lay on the ground, stunned. Then came the realization that though she was hurt, she was all right.

It took Daffy a little longer to realize that she was all right. The horse moved away hesitantly at first and then, convinced that she had gotten rid of her rider and moving deliberately, not in the headlong flight that was common to her, she went off down the trail.

Again, Amy's reaction was too slow. If only she had gotten up immediately she might have had a chance to catch Daffy, but now it was too late. She watched despondently as her horse disappeared from sight.

Cautiously Amy pulled herself into a sitting position. When she tried to stand, she was able to determine exactly where her pain was coming from—her ankle.

It wasn't crushed and probably not even broken, for she could move it. She just couldn't put any weight on it. She didn't know whether she should keep the boot on for the support it would give the ankle or take it off. There was the danger that her ankle might swell up inside the boot, and since she wanted to see what it looked like, she sat down again and as gently as possible eased the boot off.

Her ankle didn't look broken, but it was already turning blue; the pain of removing her boot let her know it was badly injured.

She leaned back against the rock. With Daffy gone, who knew where, the only way that she could get back to the ranch was to walk, but she couldn't do that either.

The idea of crawling she dismissed as quickly as it occurred to her. Crawling wouldn't get her close enough to the ranch to make any real difference, and since she was already in an open clearing, she knew she would be found eventually.

But it could be a long wait. She had told Dick that she wanted to be alone, so it might be hours before it was realized that she was missing. She hadn't even told anyone that she was taking a horse. They wouldn't have any idea she was this far from the lodge.

A short time had gone by before she thought she heard the sound of a rider. Then she distinctly heard someone calling.

"Amy! Amy!"

She gathered all her strength and yelled as loudly as she could, "Over here! Over here at the rock!"

The sound of hoofbeats became faster and closer, and within moments, Derek appeared. He was on the ground and running toward her before his horse came to a full stop.

Amy was so grateful to see him, she forgot all about the embarrassment of the night before.

"Are you all right?" he asked.

"Yes, except for my ankle. I think it's sprained," she said, pointing to her foot, which was now twice its normal size and black and blue.

"How did you know to come looking for me? I thought it would be hours before anyone knew I was missing."

"Daffy came back to the corral with her saddle half off."

"She did! You mean that silly horse didn't run away? That's great! She isn't going to be impossible to train."

Derek looked at her incredulously. "Do you realize that you are sitting here with possibly a broken ankle and all you're concerned about is that the horse who threw you came back to the stable?"

"But it wasn't like that. It was partly my own fault. I know how skittish Daffy is and I should have been paying closer attention. I let my mind wander and a rabbit spooked her."

"That was only one of your mistakes. Who gave you permission to take Daffy out alone?"

"I didn't ask anyone. You said I could handle her, and you let me ride back alone with Shannon yesterday."

"That's not the same thing. You weren't by yourself, and Dick knew to be watching for you." His eyes narrowed into slits and his voice became deeper and more ominous. "Amy, did you tell anyone you were going out on the trail?"

Amy bit her lip and had to look away from the fury in his eyes. "No," she said faintly.

Derek exploded. "That is the most irresponsible thing you could have done! It was just plain stupid! You are still a novice rider, and you shouldn't ever leave the corral unless someone is with you! Even Lisa lets someone know where she's going!"

"Okay, I was wrong about everything, but do you think you could stop yelling at me long enough to look at my ankle?"

Her words reminded him that she was hurt, and he knelt down beside her.

"What were you doing up here anyway? Taking a last look around before you left?"

"Not exactly. I came up here to try to make up my mind about what I was going to do."

Everything was suddenly so still that Derek's quiet question seemed to echo around them. "Did you?"

"Yes," she said, her voice barely above a whisper. "I've decided to stay."

Derek couldn't control the smile that tilted the corners of his mouth or the happiness that filled his heart. Slowly, he let out the breath he hadn't known he was holding.

"I knew this place would get to you eventually," he said with satisfaction.

"It wasn't just the place," Amy said. "It was mostly the people. I thought I owed it to Shannon to go back to San Francisco, but what I really owe her is my friendship. And I can be her friend from here. This is where my family is. I couldn't stand to leave them."

Derek's face was turned away from her as he studied her foot intently. Tenderly, he ran his fingers over the injured part. "Is your family the only reason?" he asked softly.

Amy smiled. "No. There is someone else. Of course, most of the time he's arguing or shouting at me, but I've grown used to it and I would miss it if I left."

Derek lowered his knee to the ground, letting his arms slide around her to gather her close. Amy could feel the powerful beating of his heart, matching her own, as he brought his lips to meet hers.

"Derek," she said when she could speak again, "I don't want you to think I've changed my mind about anything. I still think the ranch could stand a lot of improvements, and I'll do everything I can to convince Dick that I'm right."

Derek grinned as he stepped back to lift her off the ground and carry her to his horse. "I don't doubt it," he said. "I can see now that we're going to be in for some interesting arguments."

He settled her on the back of his saddle and then got on in front. As the horse started to move down the trail, Derek turned his head and spoke over his shoulder.

"This horse isn't used to carrying a double load, so he might get skittish himself. Maybe you'd better hold on tighter."

Amy saw the teasing smile on his lips and thought about arguing that she trusted him to control the horse, but she decided against it. Instead, she wound her arms around his waist and laid her cheek against his solid back.

If you've enjoyed this book...
...try four exciting First Love from Silhouette romances for 15 days—free!

These are the books that all your friends are reading and talking about, the most popular teen novels being published today. They're about things that matter most to you, with stories that mirror your innermost thoughts and feelings, and characters so real they seem like friends.

And now, we'd like to send you four exciting books to look over for 15 days—absolutely free—as your introduction to the First Love from Silhouette Book Club.℠ If you enjoy the books as much as we believe you will, keep them and pay the invoice enclosed with your trial shipment. Or return them at no charge.

As a member of the Club, you will get First Love from Silhouette books regularly—*delivered right to your home.* Four new books every month for only $1.95 each. You'll always be among the first to get them, and you'll never miss a title. There are never any delivery charges and you're under no obligation to buy anything at any time. Plus, as a special bonus, you'll receive a *free* subscription to the First Love from Silhouette Book Club newsletter!

So don't wait. To receive your four books, fill out and mail the coupon below *today!*

First Love from Silhouette

THERE'S NOTHING QUITE AS SPECIAL AS A <u>FIRST LOVE.</u>

— $1.95 —

34 ☐ THE PERFECT FIGURE March

35 ☐ PEOPLE LIKE US Haynes

36 ☐ ONE ON ONE Ketter

37 ☐ LOVE NOTE Howell

38 ☐ ALL-AMERICAN GIRL Payton

39 ☐ BE MY VALENTINE Harper

40 ☐ MY LUCKY STAR Cassiday

41 ☐ JUST FRIENDS Francis

42 ☐ PROMISES TO COME Dellin

43 ☐ A KNIGHT TO REMEMBER Martin

44 ☐ SOMEONE LIKE JEREMY VAUGHN Alexander

45 ☐ A TOUCH OF LOVE Madison

46 ☐ SEALED WITH A KISS Davis

47 ☐ THREE WEEKS OF LOVE Aks

48 ☐ SUMMER ILLUSION Manning

49 ☐ ONE OF A KIND Brett

50 ☐ STAY, SWEET LOVE Fisher

51 ☐ PRAIRIE GIRL Coy

52 ☐ A SUMMER TO REMEMBER Robertson

53 ☐ LIGHT OF MY LIFE Harper

54 ☐ PICTURE PERFECT Enfield

55 ☐ LOVE ON THE RUN Graham

56 ☐ ROMANCE IN STORE Arthur

57 ☐ SOME DAY MY PRINCE Ladd

58 ☐ DOUBLE EXPOSURE Hawkins

59 ☐ A RAINBOW FOR ALISON Johnson

60 ☐ ALABAMA MOON Cole

61 ☐ HERE COMES KARY! Dunne

62 ☐ SECRET ADMIRER Enfield

63 ☐ A NEW BEGINNING Ryan

64 ☐ MIX AND MATCH Madison

65 ☐ THE MYSTERY KISS Harper

66 ☐ UP TO DATE Sommers

67 ☐ PUPPY LOVE Harrell

68 ☐ CHANGE PARTNERS Wagner

69 ☐ ADVICE AND CONSENT Alexander

70 ☐ MORE THAN FRIENDS Stuart

71 ☐ THAT CERTAIN BOY Malek

72 ☐ LOVE AND HONORS Ryan

73 ☐ SHORT STOP FOR ROMANCE Harper

74 ☐ A PASSING GAME Sommers

75 ☐ UNDER THE MISTLETOE Mathews

76 ☐ SEND IN THE CLOWNS Youngblood

77 ☐ FREE AS A BIRD Wunsch

78 ☐ BITTERSWEET SIXTEEN Bush

79 ☐ LARGER THAN LIFE Cole

80 ☐ ENDLESS SUMMER Bayner

81 ☐ THE MOCKINGBIRD Stuart

First Love from Silhouette

82 ☐ KISS ME, KIT Francis

83 ☐ WHERE THE BOYS ARE Malek

84 ☐ SUNNY SIDE UP Grimes

85 ☐ IN THE LONG RUN Alexander

86 ☐ THE BOY NEXT DOOR Youngblood

87 ☐ ENTER, LAUGHING Leroe

88 ☐ A CHANGE OF HEART McKenna

89 ☐ BUNNY HUG Harper

90 ☐ SURF'S UP FOR LANEY Caldwell

91 ☐ R_x FOR LOVE Graham

92 ☐ JUST THE RIGHT AGE Chatterton

93 ☐ SOUTH OF THE BORDER Kingsbury

94 ☐ LEAD ON LOVE Hart

95 ☐ HEAVENS TO BITSY Harrell

96 ☐ RESEARCH FOR ROMANCE Phillips

97 ☐ LAND'S END Stuart

98 ☐ ONE OF THE GUYS Makris

99 ☐ WRITTEN IN THE STARS Marshall

100 ☐ HEAD IN THE CLOUDS Lewis

101 ☐ FIREWORKS Harper

102 ☐ SIDE BY SIDE Humphreys

103 ☐ AFTER MIDNIGHT Youngblood

104 ☐ THE FROG PRINCESS Zach

105 ☐ ONE FOR THE ROAD Hansen

106 ☐ THE FRENCH SUMMER Kay

107 ☐ HANDLE WITH CARE Marshall

108 ☐ THE LOOK OF LOVE Ladd

109 ☐ SNAP JUDGMENT Youngblood

110 ☐ CALL OF THE WILD Lewis

111 ☐ THE GIRL INSIDE Baer

112 ☐ ONCE IN CALIFORNIA Stuart

113 ☐ SEASON OF MIST Malek

114 ☐ COURTING TROUBLE Hart

115 ☐ SECRETS Enderle

116 ☐ WISHFUL THINKING Haynes

117 ☐ TURKEY TROT Elaine Harper

118 ☐ SEE YOU IN JULY Barbara Steiner

119 ☐ DON'T FENCE ME IN Brenda Cole

120 ☐ THE MAGIC CIRCLE Dorothy Francis

FIRST LOVE, Department FL/4
1230 Avenue of the Americas
New York, NY 10020

Please send me the books I have checked above. I am enclosing $_____ (please add 75¢ to cover postage and handling. NYS and NYC residents please add appropriate sales tax). Send check or money order—no cash or C.O.D.'s please. Allow six weeks for delivery.

NAME _____

ADDRESS _____

CITY _____ STATE/ZIP _____

First Love from Silhouette

Coming Next Month

Christmas Date by Elaine Harper
<u>A Blossom Valley Book</u>

The Triple A Dating Service was run by the Norwood triplets, Adam, Arthur and Amy. It was a thriving business that arranged dates for everyone but themselves. They had agreed not to mix business with pleasure. Secretly, Amy was disappointed about this. For a long time she'd had her eye on a very special boy who didn't seem to know she existed.

Lovetalk by Joyce McGill

When Jennifer agreed to tutor David Hough, she was sure that he was, as everyone said, the class "dummy." Now she wondered, could they have all been wrong? For a number of reasons, she found the possibility disturbing.

Give and Take by Ellen Leroe

How could very liberated Dani be a strong woman and still attract the macho jock with whom she had so inconveniently fallen in love? Read GIVE AND TAKE and find out!

Sugarbush Spring by Virginia Smiley

As an only child living in Vermont with her parents and grandmother, Suzie had not found her life particularly exciting. But all that changed one snowy night when the wind blew in a handsome stranger.